"If you don't mind, sir, please step out of the car." It was an order but politely given. The white policeman remained polite, but there was a firmness in his voice that showed that he wouldn't take any shit. If there was one thing Chester Hines had learned when he was a young man in his early twenties, it was not to get smart with the police—something he had learned from experience....

One of the officers opened the car door and began probing around inside the car. Seconds later he straightened up, and in his hand was the pistol Chester had tried to conceal....

Holloway House Originals by Donald Goines

DOPEFIEND
WHORESON
BLACK GANGSTER
STREET PLAYERS
WHITE MAN'S JUSTICE,
    BLACK MAN'S GRIEF
BLACK GIRL LOST
CRIME PARTNERS
CRY REVENGE
DADDY COOL
DEATH LIST
ELDORADO RED
INNER CITY HOODLUM
KENYATTA'S ESCAPE
KENYATTA'S LAST HIT
NEVER DIE ALONE
SWAMP MAN

Special Preview of *Whoreson*—page 219

WHITE MAN'S JUSTICE, BLACK MAN'S GRIEF

Donald Goines

An Original Holloway House Edition
HOLLOWAY HOUSE PUBLISHING COMPANY
LOS ANGELES, CALIFORNIA

WHITE MAN'S JUSTICE, BLACK MAN'S GRIEF

An Original Holloway House Edition

Printed in the United States of America.
Published by Holloway House Publishing Company
Los Angeles, California.

International Standard Book number: **ISBN 0-87067-885-X**

Cover photography by Jeffery
Posed by a professional model

www.hollowayhousebooks.com
or
www.hhbookstore.com

This book is for Shirley Sailor, whose love and infinite patience helped me to keep the faith and to make my editorial deadline; for the Charles and Carol Cunningham family, without whose kindness and help the pages of this novel would still be stuck in my typewriter; and for my publisher and editor, whose help and kindness I doubt I'll ever be able to repay in full. To all of them, my gratitude and thanks.

An Angry Preface

SINCE THIS WORK of fiction deals with the court system, I'd like to direct the reader's attention to an awesome abuse inflicted daily upon the less fortunate—the poor people of this country—an abuse which no statesman, judge or attorney (to my knowledge) has moved to effectively remedy. I'm speaking of the bail-bond system.

Each day, hundreds or even thousands of poor blacks and whites are picked up, arrested, booked and held in county jails all over the country until their court dates are set. The courts are glutted, and the rights of the citizen to a speedy hearing or trial are denied, owing largely to the staggering number of cases with which the courts must deal. There are cases of people (many of whom were found innocent of the charges for which they were arrested) spending more than a year in county jails simply because they couldn't raise bail-bond money. And those who are lucky enough to raise bail bond money will never get it back—even if their cases are eventually thrown out of court or if they are tried and found innocent!

Because of the overzealousness or stupidity or (and let's be honest) bigotry of some law enforcement officers, countless numbers of poor persons have to pawn their belongings, sell their cars or borrow money from finance companies (another high-interest bill they can't afford) to regain their freedom so that they can, hopefully, stay gainfully employed, only to be found not guilty as charged when their cases come up in court. Still, the poor bastards are out several hundred dollars they can ill afford—for being falsely arrested! And to poor persons, several hundred dollars represents months of food and shelter.

I'm not speaking for those who are caught breaking the law; I'm speaking for the people who are picked up on the streets or stopped for minor traffic violations and who are taken to jail on trumped-up, Catch-22 charges simply because the arresting policeman doesn't like their skin color or the way they walk or talk or dress or wear their hair.

The cities should be made to reimburse those falsely accused. They should be made to pay the bail bondsman's fee for those fortunate few who somehow raised the money for a bond, and they should be made to make monetary compensation to those who spent days, weeks or months in jail awaiting trial because they couldn't afford bail. Then and only then would the cities' taxpayers exert pressure at the upper levels, forcing policemen to use better judgment than to arrest people on ridiculous Catch-22 charges that they know will be thrown out of court.

Black people are aware of this abuse, for a disproportionate number of blacks suffer from it constantly. But black people are powerless to remedy the situation. None of our black leaders (or, I should say, so-called "black leaders") seem inclined to fight city hall over this issue—perhaps for fear of offending their white friends.

Make no mistake about it, there's big money in the bail bond business, and most of it is being made at the expense of poor blacks.

—Donald Goines, 1973

I

THE LIGHTS ON WOODWARD Avenue glistened brightly as the evening breeze blew away the last of the day's stifling heat. People walked the streets alone and in pairs, savoring relief from the blazing heat that had been their lot earlier in the day when the temperature had reached one hundred and ten in the shade.

The driver of the inconspicuous black Ford drove slowly and carefully. He didn't want any trouble before reaching his destination. That was his first mistake: driving too carefully. As he pulled towards a green light, he hesitated, then decided to speed up so that he could make the light. But as he did so, the yellow caution light came on, and again he hesitated, touching the brake, then the gas pedal, letting up to touch the brake again, then changing his mind and stomping on the gas pedal in an attempt to beat the light. Too late. The light turned red before he had reached the center of the intersection. He cursed, then stiffened when, out of the corner of his eye, he saw the patrol car parked thirty feet or so down the cross street.

Before he was completely through the intersection, he saw the squad car's headlights come on and the flashing red light. He glanced into the rearview mirror and it confirmed what he already knew. The squad car had turned the corner and was dead on his case. The thought flashed through his mind that he owed two overdue parking tickets. If they ran a make on him, he realized that his next stop would be city jail.

He removed the pistol from the shoulder holster he always wore when going out on a job, and for a second he debated the merits of trying to outrun the law. All he needed was enough time to rid himself of the gun, but the old Ford he drove didn't have the speed to outrun them. He had an extra large motor put in the car for just that purpose, but they were just too close. He glanced in the mirror and saw that they were right on his bumper.

"You better come up with something quick," he mumbled aloud, angrily. He resorted to the only thing that came to mind. He dropped the pistol to the floor and kicked it as far back under the seat as he could.

The squad car pulled up beside him, and the officer on the passenger's side waved him towards the curb. As he pulled the old Ford over he shrugged philosophically. Better that it happened now than later, he thought coldly. If it had happened on the way back, there would have been a shoot-out with no holds barred.

The policemen got out of their car and walked towards him, and he thought how easy it would be to knock them off as he pulled his wallet out and removed his driver's license. He put on his best honest-John smile, and held out the license, being helpful.

One of the officers took the license and walked slowly back towards the squad car. When that happened, the driver of the Ford knew that it was all over. They were calling in on him, doing exactly what he had hoped they wouldn't do. If he had been white, he reasoned, the chance of them doing that was small. All they would have done was write out a ticket and send him on his way, apologizing for detaining him.

In a matter of minutes the officer was back, but this time he had his hand on the butt of his gun. He nodded to his partner.

"It seems like a couple of warrants are out for you, mister," the policeman informed him quietly.

His partner had moved into position on the other side of the car. The officers worked as a unit, without bothering to speak. Each knew what the other expected from him.

"If you don't mind, sir, please step out of the car." It was an order but politely given. The white policeman remained polite, but there was a firmness in his voice that showed that he wouldn't take any shit.

If there was one thing Chester Hines had learned when he was a young man in his early twenties, it was not to get smart with police. It was something he had learned from experience. If you acted civil with them, sometimes they would treat you fairly decently.

People walking past slowed down so they could allow their curiosity to run unchecked as they watched the policemen search the well-dressed black man in the middle of the street. One of the officers opened the car door and began probing around inside the car. Seconds later he straightened up, and in his hand was the pistol Chester had tried to conceal.

The officer pulled out his handcuffs. "Okay, buddy," he drawled, watching Chester's every movement. "Turn around!" There was no disguising the disdain in his voice, and Chester turned slowly, daring not to make a quick movement, and extended his arms behind him.

"Don't make them so tight, buddy," he said as the policeman twisted the handcuffs tightly on his wrists.

"I'm not your fuckin' buddy, mack!" the policeman said harshly.

After that, Chester remained quiet, not wanting to provoke the officers of the law, and he spoke only when spoken to. When they arrived at the precinct station, he went through the mechanics of booking with a cool detachment; he'd been through the procedure so often that it had become second nature to him.

Irene! The name exploded in his mind like a burning flash—there one moment, gone the next. If it hadn't been for her goddamn nagging, he thought, he wouldn't be in the fix he was in, and he silently cursed the day he had met the tall, buxom show girl.

He had been on his honeymoon with his first wife, a large, plump beautician who owned her own beauty shop. They were honeymooning at a black resort in upper Michigan, where he had rented a small cabin for two weeks of bedding, boating and fishing—until the night he ran into Irene at the resort nightclub.

She had been one of the girls in the chorus line. Their eyes had met across the dimly lit room, and something intangible passed between them. That something grew until there was nothing for him to do but to kill his bride of two weeks. The idea wasn't new, it had been his master plan before he even married Marie, but Irene caused him to do it quicker than he had planned.

* * *

"Coffee, my man? Get it while it's hot." The trusty stood in front of his cell peering in. Chester nodded his head, not bothering to speak. He watched coldly as the man poured him a cup and pushed it beneath his steel door, through the little opening that was just large enough for a small bowl of food or cup of coffee.

"Today's your day in court, ain't it, my man?" the trusty inquired, trying to be friendly. He put his hands on his hips, which in a woman would have been sexy, but in this thin, aging homosexual, was hideously grotesque.

Chester bent down and picked up his cup, then turned his back on the trusty, not bothering to answer. In the three days he had spent in the precinct cell, he had heard the word through the grapevine that the man was a paid informer, serving his time at the county jail instead of being sent to the farm or prison. He had busted too many people, so the prison authorities feared for his life. He was too valuable to them.

Slowly Chester sipped the bitter tasting coffee. The tin cup was scorching hot. As he let the coffee cool off, he made a mental note of the informer's name: Paul Robbins. That would be a name he wouldn't forget. It always paid to know the informers, especially the professional ones. Even though Chester wasn't a dopeman, he liked to stay aware of such things. One never knew when it might just pay off.

A tall white guard stopped in front of his cell. Chester glanced up at the turnkey.

"Hines, you're going over to court in about a half an hour, so be ready," the turnkey said, then walked on down the long corridor, informing other men who were due in court.

Chester finished his coffee, rinsed out his cup, then sat down on the edge of the iron cot and let his mind continue its idle rambling. One thing was sure, he thought, he wouldn't be coming back this way. After he went to court, he'd be taken to the county jail, and if he was lucky, he'd get a chance to sleep on a mattress that night. It might not be much, but after three days on the iron cot he'd been using, it would feel like a waterbed.

There was no sense in fooling himself about bail either, he thought. That bitch of his, Irene, wouldn't be able to raise the money. Again it crossed his mind that if it hadn't been for her, he wouldn't be sitting there. Her constant nagging about money had been the main reason he had taken his pistol and left the house. True, he had been planning to knock off a whiskey store that week, but it wouldn't have been that night. Now, because he'd allowed the bitch's nagging to get on his nerves, he was on his way to court to fight a concealed weapon charge, and his funky bitch wouldn't be able to raise his bond.

With his record, he knew he didn't stand a chance in court. The judge would jam him; there was no doubt about it. But it could have been worse, he reasoned. It could have happened after he stuck up the store, then his ass would have really been fucked up. Instead of just a c-c-w to fight, he'd have had an armed robbery on his back, and that would have meant *big* trouble.

Taking his time, Chester dressed in the clothes his wife had left downstairs for him. He didn't have a mirror, but he knew that the tight black pants fit him nicely. He still had a small waist even though he was in his late thirties. The only things that showed his age were the circles under his eyes and the bags that had formed there from keeping late hours. He put on his white shirt; then, as he heard the guard opening the doors, he slipped on his sports coat. In minutes the turnkey was in front of his cell.

The men lined up against the wall. Two more guards came along and handcuffed the men two abreast. For something to do, Chester counted the men in the line. There were ten other doomed asses, he told himself, as he wondered how many of them had spent half the celibate years in prison that he had served during his life of crime.

The guard came back and ran a thin chain down between them, making them all chained to the same piece.

"Goddamn it," the man handcuffed to Chester began, "this is the one thing I hate about this shit! They chain you up like you're a fuckin' dog or something!"

"What do you expect?" Chester replied. "If they didn't take precautions and chain you, when they walked us through the tunnel they'd have to have fifty guards out there to keep the guys from running."

"Well I sure as hell wouldn't run," the man answered. "I ain't did nothing, not a goddamn thing no way. They got me down here for nothin'! These white folks just fuck over a man, if you ask me."

"I didn't ask you," Chester said under his breath, then decided to ignore the man. He had seen too many like him. Always talking about their innocence. And besides, he didn't feel in the mood for loose conversation. His mind was too occupied with his appointment with the judge. Maybe, just maybe, he hoped, the judge might give him probation. Since he hadn't been arrested in the past two years, it just might go in his favor. He just as quickly laughed the idea away.

That was something he could forget. He'd never been that lucky before, so there was no reason to start hoping for a miracle now.

"What's so goddamn funny?" His handcuffed partner inquired, his voice full of self-righteous anger, as the line of men started shuffling along.

Chester glanced around at the heavyset, dark-complexioned man handcuffed to him. "Nothing that you'd understand, brother, nothing at all," he said quietly.

"You guys keep the fuckin' noise down! You're not on your way to a private dance or something," the tall red-faced guard leading the way yelled over his shoulder.

"We're not on our way to a goddamn funeral, either," a short well dressed black man yelled back at him.

The group reached an elevator marked for prisoners only. The line of men stopped. Two more white guards joined the first group, then they began the job of loading the men into the small elevator. The men on the front of the chain went in first and walked around inside the tiny elevator, making a complete circle and stopping in front of the elevator door. The men were loaded into the tight space like cattle. The guards were no better off; they had to squeeze inside themselves.

"Get off my goddamn foot, motherfucker!" someone in the rear yelled angrily. No sooner had the elevator doors closed, when the tightly packed bodies sucked up all the available oxygen. Chester fought to breathe. He thought he would suffocate inside the tiny space. He raised his head high, sucking at the stale air that seemed thick enough to cut with a knife. The odors from the unwashed bodies filled his nostrils, and he decided to hold his breath. Better to suffocate, he reasoned, than to die from an overload of funk. The elevator finally stopped. The guards stepped out quickly; they, too, wanted to escape from the strong odor and lack of air.

The walk through the tunnel was quick. Every now and then they would pass another guard, strategically placed so that the chain of men would be under constant observation. There were desperate men in the small group of prisoners. Some of them were fighting murder charges, and any opportunity to escape would set them in violent motion.

The precautions that the guards took showed that they anticipated all forms of trouble and meant to handle it if it should jump off. When they came out of the tunnel, the men were separated from the chain that held them all together. They were still handcuffed, two abreast, though. As they were released from the chain, they were led off to small bull pens—depending upon what judge they were going before. The petty cases, misdemeanors and traffic violations were separated from what they termed the hardened crooks, the violent men.

Chester studied the faces around him. Some of them couldn't hide the fear in their eyes. They were terrified, and one could see the fear jumping out of their eyes. Their legs shook uncontrollably. One young boy had pissed on himself. Whenever anyone happened to catch his eye, he looked away or glanced down at the floor.

The guard pushed Chester and his chained partner over towards one of the bull-pen doors. He took out his keys and unlocked the handcuffs, then opened the large steel door. He beckoned for them to go inside. "You boys know the routine, so hop to it." He slammed the door behind them. Before Chester could find a place to sit down, the strong, heavy, steel door opened again, and another two men came stumbling in.

"Keep your fucking hands off me, screw!" one of the men cursed over his shoulder at the guard who had pushed him.

The two small benches inside the bull pen were already occupied, so Chester, after wiping off a spot on the floor, sat down. He knew that he probably had a two-hour wait before court opened. They always brought the prisoners over early in the morning, at least two hours before court convened. Chester wrinkled his nose and moved. He had sat down too close to the piss hole, a small hole in the floor that the men had to use for a toilet. The smell coming from it was enough to turn a person's stomach. Around the small hole was dried vomit that someone had had the decency to try to deposit in the hole, instead of just anywhere in the bull pen. There were spots in the corners where some men hadn't been so considerate, and at that moment, another started to piss up against the wall. The men sitting near him cursed loudly, but the man continued to piss. The urine ran down the wall, and a small stream of it began to flow across the floor.

"You better hope, nigger, that that piss of yours has eyes, 'cause if it gets on me, I'm kickin' you in your ass!" A short, young, black man growled at the older man who had pissed against the wall. The young man continued: "You can damn well bet they got you in the right place, you sorry motherfucker." He moved away from the spot where he had been sitting. The small stream of urine hadn't reached him, but it was getting within a couple of feet from where he had been sitting.

He paced up and down the bull pen, glaring at the man who had pissed. "I should make you get down on your knees and lick that shit up. You don't give a fuck noway. It don't make you no difference that other men have to come behind you and use this same fuckin' place. No." The more he talked, the angrier he became. The large muscles in his arm jumped, and from the looks of him, he was quite capable of doing just what he threatened.

"Now wait a minute, blood. I didn't mean no harm," the drunk said, trying to justify his action.

"No harm my ass!" the young blood replied. "It don't even cross your mind that the men that come in here after us might have to sit in that funky piss of yours. You ornery motherfucker. You could have walked over and pissed in the hole, just like the rest of the men. But no, hell no, you had to piss on the floor." Blood stopped in front of the drunk. "You know what you are, man? You're a self-centered, cruel, no-good bastard whose own mammy don't want him."

"Wait a minute, blood, don't talk about my poor old maw," the drunk said. Before he could add another word, the young man slapped him twice across the face, viciously. The sound reverberated through the bull pen and empty halls. "Now, you motherfucker, take your shirt off and wipe up that shit." The young man didn't crack a smile. His eyes were cold and his lips were pulled down in a violent sneer.

The other men fell silent. When they finally spoke, they spoke in whispers, as though they were afraid they might bring violence down on their own heads. Chester grinned as he watched the man wipe up the piss with his shirt but soon grew tired of watching and looked inward, filled with his own worries.

2

THE SOUND OF THE KEY in the lock caused all of the men in the bull pen to glance up at the door. The door swung open, revealing a guard, clipboard in hand. He stayed in the hallway, a few feet from the threshold, to avoid the bull pen's smell as he called out names: "Rufus Johnson, Billy Jones, John Caster, Donald Warren, James Sailor, Jim Jackson, Tony Towasand...."

He continued calling names in a bored, slightly nasal monotone and, as he did so, the men formed a line at the door. Chester was the last to be called, and he formed the end of the line and followed the men out into the hallway. Guards stood at each end of the

corridor, holding shotguns, as the prisoners were led
down the short hall. The guard that opened their door
was the only one who didn't have a weapon of any
kind. He led the men up to a huge oak door, where
he stopped and removed his keys. When he opened
the door for the men, he made sure they went in sin-
gle file.

Chester blinked at the harsh light in the courtroom
and peered around curiously. He had been in and out
of courtrooms all his life, but he never got over his
fear of them. The black-robed men who sat up high
on the benches dispensing their so-called "justice"
filled him with awe. It was not a feeling of reverence
or of wonder caused by something sublime. It was a
feeling of terror, inspired by the raw power that these
hypocrites held over the helpless black men who came
before them. He didn't fear the men themselves. He
knew well that they were insignificant, even while
recognizing how insidious they could sometimes be.
He feared the power, the power of life and death these
men held in their hands. Half of them were too old
to keep up with the times; they tried to beat down the
complexities of the seventies with their gavels, with
their twenties- and thirties-spawned attitudes, with
raw power.

The courtroom was full of people. The seats were
filled with men in custody and with people who came
to watch the wretched human beings squirm before
the all powerful judges.

The line that Chester was in seemed endless as he
stared over the heads of most of the black men in front

of him. He started counting. There were thirty men in front of him, and out of that thirty, only three were white. Two of the white men had the look of the derelict about them.

The line moved faster than Chester thought it would. It seemed like only minutes before he was almost in front of the judge. The black man he had been chained to as they came through the tunnel stepped before the judge. As his charge was read off, Chester had to fight back a grin.

A large hardened black woman got up and came forward, pushing a young girl eleven years old down the aisle in front of her. Chester examined the young girl closely. Take the braids out of her hair and let it down and she'd definitely look older. Her young breasts were large and firm. She was overripe, even if she was under age.

"Is this the child that the accused is supposed to have molested?" the judge asked as he leaned down to get a better view of the young girl's breasts.

Chester watched the gleam in the old, gray-haired judge's eyes and knew without a doubt what the man was thinking. How was it? He'd probably give up his front seat in hell for a shot of that young black pussy, Chester reflected coldly as he watched the proceedings.

"Ain't no *supposed* to it!" the older woman screamed hotly. "I come home from work and when I entered the front door I could hear this child screaming her head off. Right then and there I dropped them bags I'd been carrying and run to help her. At first

I'm thinkin' the child done burned herself or something, but when I reached the back of the house, I see this bastard with his pants down and his goddamn thing in his hand!" As she related the incident, her voice rose several octaves until she was almost screeching at the judge.

The judge didn't bother to reprimand her for speaking out or swearing. He just nodded his head, then set a five thousand dollar bond on the man. As the accused tried to explain, one of the court-appointed policemen rushed him away from the judge.

The courtroom had fallen silent as the woman spoke. Now, with that case out of the way, the judge paused to drink a glass of water, which was poured by an attractive young white girl who kept going back and forth bringing him the different files on the men and women who had to appear before him. While they waited for the next case to come up, the people in the courtroom gossiped.

Chester wiped the sweat from his brow as he stepped in front of the judge. Since the baby raper only got a five thousand dollar bond, he reasoned, he stood a good chance of getting a low bond. His case was nowhere near as bad as the man who had preceded him.

He waited silently while the judge read off his record.

It took awhile because he had a long record.

"What were you doing with a gun in your car, Mister Hines?" Before Chester could reply, the judge continued, "From your record, sir, you're not supposed to even have a weapon at your home, let alone in your car." He stared down silently for a brief moment." I see by your record you once killed a man," he said, holding up his hand to cut off Chester's reply. "Yes, I can see here where you were released on justified homicide, but if you hadn't had a gun on that occasion, you wouldn't have taken a man's life."

"If I wouldn't have had a gun at that time, your honor, I wouldn't be standing here now. I'd be dead." In the short silence that followed, Chester decided that, if he were ever going to get anything said, he had better start saying it now. "Your honor, if the court will allow, I've been just recently married and I've just gotten a good job. If you would give me a personal bond, sir, I'm sure I'd be able to afford the money to hire me a lawyer for this case."

"I'm sure you would hire yourself a good lawyer, Mister Hines. Your kind of man always seems to hire the best lawyer around," the judge stated sharply, then added, "but from your record, sir, it would be a travesty of justice if I were to allow you out on a personal bond. Ten thousand dollars, with two securities," the judge stated, then hit the block with his small gavel, his way of informing the court guards that he was finished with the case and was ready for the next. While Chester had stood before the judge, the court officers had been busy. There was a new line of men behind Chester, all waiting for their chance in court.

Chester stared up at the judge, dumbfounded. He hadn't expected the stiff decision. It was too much. He'd never get out on bond now. Even if his wife

came up with the money, she'd never be able to raise
the two securities. He turned around and searched the
sea of faces in the courtroom. His wife and kids were
sitting three rows back. Tears were rolling down her
cheeks as she stared at him. She had been in enough
courtrooms to know just what the judge had done.
There were few black men who could come up with
the thousand dollars cash it would take, plus he'd need
someone to put up a house for one of the securities.
It was impossible, and his wife believed in her heart
the judge knew that when he had set the bond.

An officer grabbed Chester's arm firmly and guided him from the courtroom. He walked along in a
slight daze. It had happened. Even though he had
thought that it would be hard, he hadn't really given
up hope of making a small bond, something that he
might have been able to raise, even if his wife had to
sell the car.

When they reached the corridor, he jerked his arm
from the policeman's grip. "Goddamn it! I can walk.
You don't have to shove me," he yelled belligerently
into the officer's face.

"Just take it easy," the officer said lightly. "I didn't
set your bond, and I'm just doing my job."

"Okay, okay, just don't shove me," Chester said as
he regained control. "How's chances of me seeing my
wife and kids for a minute, officer?"

The young officer looked at him slowly. He was
young, but since the two years he had worked in the
courtroom, he had seen all kinds of men. To him,
Chester had gotten a raw deal. He saw dozens of c-

c-w cases come through the courtroom, and he knew that had Chester been white, he'd have been given a small bond or released on his own personal word. If not a personal bond, it wouldn't have been higher than a five hundred dollar bond—something a man could raise without ruining himself. It was a cold world, the guard thought, and if you were black, it was more than cold—it was pure hell. The guard thought about Chester's having killed a man before, but he reasoned that Chester had been tried and released, so there was no reason for him to have to pay for it now. But from what he knew about the court system, he'd be willing to bet that every time Chester ended up in court, he'd still be paying for that not-guilty verdict.

"This way," the guard finally said and led him down another corridor. They walked in silence until the guard stopped in front of another bull pen. On this steel door, there was a wire window where the prisoners could talk to their lawyers or other visitors. "I'll try to get your wife back here for a few minutes before they take you over to the county jail. Just have patience," the guard said as he opened the door.

Chester entered the small cell and glanced around. It was identical to the one he had been in earlier, only this one didn't have the strong odor the other one had, and it was smaller. There were only four men inside, and each one stayed off to himself. A tall white man paced back and forth. Each time footsteps were heard in the hallway, he'd rush to the front of the cell and try to see out of the small wire window. Once he yelled out to a passing guard, "Get me a bondsman back here, mack, and I'll give you fifty dollars."

Finally the guard arrived, leading the way for Irene. She followed the guard, pulling two small girls along behind her. Both of the little girls were crying.

Chester pushed his face against the wire window. "Hi, baby. Looks like you goin' have to make it without your old man for a while," he said casually, trying to make it easy for her. The kids were too small to see their father, and both of them started to yell when they heard his voice.

Irene bent down and lifted one of them up. After a few seconds, in which Chester tried to kiss the little girl through the wire, she lifted the other one up. They talked for a few moments, but there was nothing Chester could tell her to do. It was all cut and dried.

"Listen, baby, ain't no sense worrying. I'm on my way to prison, anyway, so whatever time I do in the county jail now will be just the less time I'll have to do in prison. It ain't dead time no more like it used to be. Now, they give a man all the time he spends in the county jail. So just keep your head up."

She tried to grin at him. "I ain't worried, baby. Things might work out better than you think. You'll go before another judge for sentence, so you might just get a break. That's what the guard says. After you spend some time in the county jail, it will all go in your favor."

"Don't fool yourself, Irene. All these fuckin' ass judges are just alike. The black ones are just as bad as the white ones or worse. I don't know if I'd rather take my chances with a white one instead of those ass kissin' black ones. They're so scared that their white friends might think they're giving a black man a break, they lean over backwards to give a nigger some time. No, baby, with my record, the shit's in the fan."

"Well, honey, it could have been worse, couldn't it?" she asked. They both knew what she meant. They kept no secrets from each other; she knew he was a stick-up man and professional killer. It could have been worse. At his age he couldn't stand one of those twenty to twenty-five prison sentences.

He shook his head in agreement. He had told her many times that, if he got busted on a robbery, he'd hold court in the streets before he'd let the police take him on an armed robbery charge. "Yeah baby, it could have been much worse, so that's one reason why I'm thankful. It's only a concealed weapon charge, and the most I'm looking forward to is maybe two years. I'll be out sometime next year, maybe."

The guard came back down the corridor. "Well, miss, I'm afraid that's as long as I can allow. I've got too many other prisoners to worry about today, so I'll have to take you back up front."

The tall white man tapped Chester on the shoulder. "Hey, fellow, how about having your wife give my name to a bondsman for me? If she does, I'll send up fifty dollars for you, I swear."

"What's your name, buddy? I'll give it to her, even though I know goddamn well you ain't goin' send me no fifty dollars." Chester gave her the inmate's name and told her to try and send a bondsman back there immediately.

Irene turned and stared angrily at the young guard who had tapped her on the shoulder. Before she could say something nasty, Chester intervened. "It's all right, honey. If he had wanted to, he could have stopped you from coming back here to see me. He's all right, and I appreciate the favor he did me by allowing you the little bit of time he did. Now don't forget," he said, speaking loud enough for the other men to hear, "be sure to send the bondsman back here for Edward Binns. Be sure to tell him to come as soon as possible."

"Okay, daddy," she replied, then grabbed the little girls' hands and brushed past the waiting officer. He followed behind, shrugging his shoulders. It was something he was used to. The women always seemed to act as if it was his fault. As he followed her, prisoners called out to him to allow them the use of the phone or for other things, from buying them a cup of coffee to find a bondsman for them; he only shrugged and kept on walking.

After Irene left, Chester settled back to wait until they came to take him back across the street. Edward Binns stopped and inquired, "Do you really think your wife will do that for me? I mean, do you think she'll take the time to find a bondsman?"

For a brief second, Chester studied the man. He didn't bother to tell him that it wouldn't take her a minute to stop in the hallway and approach one of the dozens of bondsmen who ran up and down the corridor. "Yeah, man. I told her about the fifty dollars you promised me, so she'll be sure and send one. But what about the fifty? When am I supposed to get that? Next week on your payday or some other bullshit like that?"

"No, no, nothing like that," the man said, reaching in his pocket and pulling out his money. "See, I have it here. I'll be sure to give it to you. In fact, I'll be damn glad to give it to you if she sends that bondsman."

Chester grinned. He hadn't believed the man at first, and now he couldn't believe the man was that square. "How did you happen to get locked up, Ed?" he asked out of curiosity.

"It's all a mistake. It's a nonsupport case. But actually, they've got the wrong Edward Binns. They want an Edward Bimms, not Binns. But that fucking judge wouldn't even listen. So I didn't have the time to get in touch with my lawyer or a bondsman."

Chester laughed loudly. "Yeah, man, I know what you mean. That goddamn judge ain't got the time or sense to listen to whatever anyone might have to say. He thinks he's God or something."

"Edward Binns? Is there an Edward Binns in there?" a short, white-haired man asked through the window.

"Yes, yes," Edward yelled as he rushed towards the door. "I'm the man you're looking for."

Chester moved close to the door, protecting his fifty dollar investment in case Irene had sent the man back.

"A young colored woman said you needed a bondsman, sir. Is that correct?"

The other men inside the cell watched coldly as

Chester collected the easy fifty dollars. Some of them frowned, but it didn't make a damn bit of difference to Chester as he collected his money and took his time folding it up so that they could see him doing it. He laughed harshly at the frowns, but it was part of life. A few nights ago, if he had had this much money in his pocket, he wouldn't have been pressed to go out into the streets to commit a crime. Now, here in jail, he ran into the money without even thinking about it. It was a gift, a bird nest on the ground. Oh well, he reasoned, it would make his stay in the county jail a lot more pleasant. Now he wouldn't have to worry about cigarettes or candy or other small things that made prison bearable.

The sound of the guards coming, carrying chains, brought him back to reality.

3

IT HAD BEEN AN overwhelmingly exasperating day, and it wasn't finished yet. The long line of prisoners had finally been brought over to the basement of the county jail, where after arriving the men and women had been put in separate cells. There were eight long concrete cells, seven of them belonged to the men, the eighth reserved for the women. Each cell door was operated by a master control. One deputy sat in a bulletproof compartment where he could see everything that went on in the basement. The area was horseshoe shaped. In the center, the other deputies sat at their desks, taking care of the paperwork, when they weren't taking the chains off new prisoners and assigning them to various cells. These were only temporary arrangements. The prisoners were held in the basement only until they were assigned to one of the wards, starting from the second floor up. The women were kept on the sixth floor, while the men occupied the others.

Chester sat on the cold iron bench, weary and tired of the waiting. All he wanted now was to be taken up to the ward that would be his home for the next few months. He tried to tell himself that he shouldn't be impatient, because once they did take him upstairs, it would be the last time he'd get out for quite a while. Many of the prisoners looked forward to being taken across the street to court; they knew that it would take all day and that they would get a chance to gossip with old friends that they hadn't seen for months or years. But Chester hadn't reached that stage of boredom yet; he didn't find sitting around in a bull pen gratifying. He didn't give a damn about the other men, really. He was tired of hearing the same question: "What they got you for, my man?"

The sounds from the kitchen, a portable wagon with food on it, informed the waiting men that it wouldn't be long now. That's what the wait was always about. They always fed the men when they came back from court, because they knew the men would have been across the street in court all day without even a drink of water.

They took the women out first. Men rushed to the front of the cells to stare at the women. Some of them acted as though they hadn't seen women for years,

and in some of the cases, it was almost true. Some of
the men had been in the county jail for over a year
waiting to go to court, and if they didn't get any visitors, they didn't have an opportunity to see a woman.
But most of the men were just off the streets, so it
didn't really make any sense to Chester that they
crowded against the bars, staring at the women prisoners.

The men kept up a steady flow of pleasant insults
towards the women: "Hey, honey, pull your skirt up
a little. Let me get a glimpse of that thing. Hey,
momma, you with the mini on. Bend down, honey, so
that I can see the cheeks of them buns."

"Knock that shit off!" a deputy yelled, knowing that
he wouldn't be obeyed. The only recourse the deputies
had was to rush the women through. The longer the
women dallied, the louder the verbal exchanges. The
women were just as bad as the men. Some of them
actually enjoyed it, or seemed to.

The young man who had slapped the drunk earlier
sat down next to Chester. "My name's Willie Brown,
brother. Looks as if you and I are going to be visitors
of this fine establishment for quite a while."

"You could get odds on with that bet, Willie,"
Chester replied quietly. "My name's Chester Hines,
brother. It looks like the judges wanted to make sure
they had plenty men. They must need some help up
at the prison for pickin' and shit. It's that time of the
year, or it will be by the time most of us go back to
court for sentencing."

Willie laughed. "Yeah, man, they need something.

But this goddamn place is already overcrowded. They tell me they got them sleeping on the floors upstairs. I was talking to that brother over there," he said, nodding his head in the direction of a light-complexioned Negro. "The brother says there is only eighteen bunks in his ward, and they got twenty-four men in there."

With his agile mind, it didn't take any complicated thought for Chester to realize what that meant. If one ward was overcrowded like that, it meant all of them were. Because wherever there was an empty bed, they would put a man. If six men had to sleep on the floor, then every ward had the same problem.

The deputies led the women away. In minutes, two of them were back, and they started to unlock the men's cells, taking them one at a time. Each man stood in line until a trusty gave him a tin bowl with all of his food mixed up in it together. No matter what they had, it was always fed to them in a bowl. Two slices of bread were on top of the food.

Chester and Willie stuck together. For some reason the young man seemed to take a liking to Chester. They stood in line, speaking softly to each other, neither man bothering to impose on the other by crying about his case. They finally reached the food wagon and Chester received his bowl of food. He glanced at the noodles floating around in the lukewarm supposed-to-be soup. The bread was semi-hard, but he knew from past experience that the only way to make it in the county was to try and eat a little of everything you got, until you caught up with the wagon, and by then, it might be just sold out of everything but cigarettes. Sometimes they were even out of those, too.

"From my long association with this fine establishment, Willie, I can definitely inform you that, if you have any resistance to the food in your bowl, don't throw it away. Whatever ward we land on, there will be some hungry soul who might just buy it from you for a candy bar or something else you might like. Sometimes they have pies that they've gotten off the wagon."

"Yeah, brother, I'm hip to it. To my regret, I hate to inform you, I've visited this free hotel before. Though at the time, I didn't have any plans of returning soon. But that's life. You never know about such things."

"All right, you guys, keep that noise down. You're not at a private resort, you know," one of the deputies yelled at them.

Before eating, the men were loaded in an elevator and taken upstairs. This time the elevator was not loaded to its capacity, and the men were not handcuffed. There was nowhere for them to run. Nearly all the doors operated by control of the master buttons, and there were deputies on each floor—well out of reach of the prisoners—sitting in their bulletproof control rooms.

As the elevator stopped on the fourth floor, each man stepped out carrying his bowl of food. "Maybe if we're lucky, Willie, we might get put in the same ward. I'll be able to teach you how to play chess, then."

"I hope so, Chester. I'd like to learn the game. Besides, I like to hear you rap, man. You seem to have a lot on the ball."

There were eight men altogether. As the guard opened the door, he spoke to the men: "You boys are pretty lucky. This is the new ward. Some of the boys ain't got it that good. They'll have to go to the old part of the jail, but you guys get to stay in the brand new compartments." He laughed loudly as he impatiently swung the door wide and walked in, shuffling the cards he held in his hands.

It was a long corridor leading down past four cells. When the deputy stopped at the first cell, the men inside set up a howl. "Don't put none in here, man, we ain't got no damn room. It ain't but fourteen beds in here, and we already got twenty men! Where the fuck do you think they goin' sleep?"

With difficulty, the guard managed to control his anger. "How the fuck do I know where they goin' sleep? The judge sent them over, goddamn it, so you might as well make room." He called out two names, then yelled back to the guard standing in the hallway. "Break number one, two going in."

The men inside the cell began to curse loudly. Chester stared in the new cellblock. If these were the new cells, he sure didn't want any part of it. Each was a large open bay, with double bunks strung out in a circle around it. The back of it was bars, just like the front, so that the deputies could walk up and down the catwalks at night without fear of being grabbed and held hostage. Against the tiny wall that was like a box, with the shower inserted inside of it, was the toilet; it sat out in plain view. Right next to it was the table where everybody had to eat. It was clean, but whenever a man had to shit, the men playing cards at the table would have to put up with the smell or quit playing until he finished.

Chester turned to the deputy. "If by chance you're overcrowded, turnkey, how's the chances of a man getting locked up in the old side. If I've got to jail I'd like to be around the old surroundings. They bring back such memories, you know."

The deputy laughed. "Yeah, mac, I know just what you mean. These new compartments seem to have that effect on just about everybody who comes up here. Especially if they've had the opportunity to have visited the old side."

"Close number one!" the turnkey yelled and walked on down the rock towards the next ward. The prisoners followed behind dejectedly. The sight of number one had taken the heart out of them.

When they reached number two, a man lying on a bunk glanced up and yelled, "Put them white boys in here, dep." The colored deputy glanced out of the corner of his eye at the two white prisoners.

Chester watched the proceedings, amused. He glanced into the ward and noticed that it was just as crowded as the first one, but there was one difference. The first cell had been full, but there had only been black men in it. This one had four white prisoners in it, and they all had one thing in common. Each man sported a black eye.

The deputy knew as well as Chester what was happening. From past experience Chester knew. The white boys were being fucked, and their food and money were being taken. It happened on every ward. Whenever possible, the turnkeys tried to make it equal. If twenty men were in a cell, they tried to make it ten white and ten black. But it was impossible. For one thing, the whites made bond as soon as possible. Either their people were able to raise the money or their bonds weren't as high as the average black man's. Either way, whichever whitey was unfortunate enough to have to spend some time in the county jail, it was an experience he would never forget. The loss of his manhood was only the beginning. The loss of his life was a good possibility. The only ones who were ever spared were those who had done time or who knew the ropes or who could talk like a brother and fight as good as one, too. There was absolutely no two ways about it, a white boy had to fight to save his asshole.

The deputy hesitated, then called out, "Break number two!" The door slid open quietly. That was one thing it had on the old side, Chester thought coldly, and about the only thing. The damn doors didn't make any noise.

The black men inside the cell crowded towards the front. "If they come in here, I want the blond," a thin black boy in his early teens said loudly.

"You guys fuck with these prisoners," the deputy said angrily, "and your asses are going to be in more trouble than you're already in!" He didn't even have to glance at the cards to tell the white prisoners that this was where they were assigned. He knew that the white deputy on the desk had tried to assign them where other white boys were, and this was it. He did glance at the cards to get their names, though. "Okay you two, in there," he said.

The two white kids looked at each other nervously. "Man, I ain't going in that fuckin' place! You can take me to the goddamn hole, but I ain't going in there," the taller of the two said.

"All right, buddy, come on," one of the black prisoners in the cell said. "It ain't as bad as that. The guys were just foolin' you. Come on in. You see we got some other white boys in here."

The deputy stared at the Negro angrily. "You. Get your shit," he said loudly, then he pointed at the black man who had first asked him to put the white boys inside the cell. "You too. Get your shit, both of you are moving." He twisted his head around and glanced at the prisoners behind him. The closest men to him were Chester and Willie. "What's your name?" he said and pointed a pencil at Chester.

"Chester Hines." The answer was sharp and to the point.

"You aren't afraid to go in there, are you, mac?" The deputy inquired, knowing the answer before even asking the question. Chester didn't bother to answer, he just stepped past the two white boys and walked inside the cell.

"Since you're doing me such a favor, deputy, don't forget my partner there," he said, pointing towards

Willie.

Willie laughed and didn't even wait for the guard.
He yelled his name back over his shoulder, "Willie
Brown is my white folks name; Kenyata is my black
name, deputy. Use whichever one you want," he said
as he stepped inside the cell.

The deputy wiped sweat from his brow. "I thought
I told you guys to get your shit together." he said loudly.

"Man, we ain't did nothing—have we, fellers?"
They turned to the men inside the ward, but no one
spoke up in their behalf.

"I ain't askin' you again," the deputy said, his voice
revealing anger.

The two men started to pick up their meager
belongings. As each man moved around his bunk,
Chester pulled Willie over and whispered in his ear.
"Listen, baby boy, if you don't want to sleep on the
floor, this is what we goin' have to do. As soon as
the deputy moves away from the door, we take over
the two bunks that they left. We got one thing in our
favor—they were bunking together, so we can do the
same thing. Either you take the top or the bottom. It
don't make no difference, just as long as we get a
bunk. Don't make no sense us sleeping on the goddamn floor."

Willie shook his head in agreement. "We might
have a little trouble out of some of these niggers,
man." Chester studied the man he was talking to.
There was no fear there.

"You ain't worried about it, are you, blood?"

Chester asked quietly.

"Close number two!" the deputy yelled. The two men who were put out of the ward followed behind the deputy, cursing.

For an answer to Chester's question, Willie moved over and jumped up on the top bunk. Chester was right behind him.

As they commandeered the bunks, the other men in the cell who had been sleeping on the floor began to yell. "Hey, man, ya cain't take them beds. We been waiting weeks for an opening." Three of the men lying on the floor got up and walked towards Chester and Willie.

Willie jumped from his bunk quickly, landing next to Chester.

"Listen, baby and I ain't goin' tell you but once," Chester began. "These bunks ain't empty, and they weren't goin' be empty, you dig? The guys that stayed here wasn't about to go home, so you weren't goin' to get them noway. Now, they took us from our bunks and brought us down here to exchange places with them guys, so that's what we're doin'. They goin' get our bunks, and we got theirs." Chester stared the men in the eye. He was taller than all three of them, but they were younger. Two of them were black, while one of them was white. He glared at the Negroes. He knew if any trouble came, it would come from them.

"Man, you ain't got to explain anything to them niggers!" Willie said, pulling his shirt off. The muscles on his arms jumped. Even though he was short, he was so husky that he looked like a young bull in his prime.

One of the young brothers in front backed up to make sure he wouldn't be in front if a fight broke out. The rest of the men just watched. What would happen now would be a case of the strongest winning out. The men at the rear of the line for a bunk would try and take the place of those at the top. If the top men were weak, they would lose out.

The men who already had bunks were thankful the new men didn't come in and try and take theirs. It happened like that at times. If a real gorilla came in, he would look around, pick his mark, then make his move. Either the man who owned the bunk fought or gave it up. He'd have to do one or the other.

After several tense seconds, the men backed off.

Chester relaxed and sat back on the bunk. It was over; they had won. Willie sat down beside him. "Well, big bro, looks like the first round goes to us, don't it?"

"You can bet on it, Willie. As long as we're in here, we're going to win all of them. You can bet on that, too."

4

LATER THAT EVENING, Chester and Willie found out that they had not only bluffed the weak ones in the ward but had gained the respect of the strong ones as well, so they fit right in. They waited until the evening meal before the dogs in the ward showed their hands. Then the action was directed towards the two white boys. Hot dogs were served for the evening meal, and as the white boys came back carrying their trays, four black inmates stopped them.

"You see that?" one of the men pointed out to the two white boys. The boys turned their heads and watched as four other white boys on the ward took their trays around, each one of them taking the hot dogs from his tray and giving them to the black inmates. One of the white boys came over to the crowd.

"Hey Jesse, how about me keepin' one of these, since you goin' get theirs too?" he asked, nodding towards the new white inmates as he held out his tray for Jesse to take the hot dogs from it.

Jesse, a tall, brown-skinned black man, stared hard at the thin white boy. "I'll go along with it this time, Mike, but don't make it no habit." He pushed one of the hot dogs back on Mike's tray.

The small, undernourished looking white boy grinned as if a big favor had been done for him. He flashed his hot dog in front of his friends, not saying in words what his action meant: Look what I got, fellers; don't you wish you had one too? And they did wish they had one, because none of them had been that fortunate.

"What's your name, boy?" Jesse asked sharply, sticking his finger in the boy's face.

"My friends call me Tony," the boy answered just as sharply. He had nerve, but he was outnumbered almost three to one. His friend wasn't any help at all.

"Here, man," his partner said quickly. "You can have my hot dogs. I ain't hungry noway." He held out his food. "Take it all, man, I don't want none of it."

Tony spoke for his friend. "Leave him something, man. He gave you his hot dogs, so leave the potatoes for him. Don't be silly, Gene, how long you think we're going to be here? Just for a day or something?"

The man who had taken his food refused to give

back the potatoes. Tony glared at him. "What are you, man, some kind of a fucking animal? You act like you're not used to eating."

Chester laughed. He liked the white boy's nerve, but that was as far as he'd allow himself to go. He didn't want to get into it one way or another. It was up to the white boys to get themselves out of it. If they really put up enough of a struggle, they could pull it off. All they needed was the help of the other white boys. There were only a few asshole bandits in the ward, and most of them were cowards. If they didn't have a pack behind their backs, they wouldn't do anything by themselves.

Tony walked over near the toilet and quickly tossed his hot dogs into the stool. "Now, if you want them, get them out of the shitter," he said coldly and sat down and began eating the rest of his food.

Chester laughed loudly again. One of the men asked him sharply, "What's so goddamn funny?"

"You, punk!" Chester snarled and his eyes had turned a cold, freezing, jet black. "Now if you want some more hot dogs, here are a few you might be able to get if you're man enough to take them."

Willie laughed too. "Yeah, baby, if you're hungry enough, I guess you might as well go for broke."

Tony split the rest of the food with his friend. The other white boys in the ward just watched, afraid to say anything.

Later on that night, after the trays had been picked up, Jesse walked over to where Willie and Chester were sitting. "Say my man," he said, "I ain't trying to be funny, but tell me something. You guys happen to be friends of those two ofays or something?"

"No, baby, it ain't nothing like that." Willie answered quickly. "What you and them do is your affair." He glanced at Chester to see how he was taking it. Chester nodded in agreement.

"Okay then," Jesse replied, " 'cause we goin' have us a little fun tonight, and we didn't want to be steppin' on anybody's toes—if you know what I mean."

"Yeah, man, we know just what you mean," Chester said quietly. He knew just what the man meant. They were getting ready to have a little rape party and didn't want any interference.

Jesse walked away and stopped beside the white boys. "You boys are new to this rock, so I'll tell you the rules. We make all the new guys take a shower, so you two had better start getting ready, if you don't want to end up taking it with your clothes on."

"Is that right?" Tony asked, and from the sound of his voice one could tell he knew just what was about to come off. His partner, Gene, didn't though. He stepped right into the trap.

"Yeah, man," Gene said, eager to be accepted by the group, "that won't be any trouble. I was wanting to take a bath anyway. Do they have any soap a person can use?"

He looked around in bewilderment when the others broke out laughing at his gullibility. One of the prisoners tossed him a bar of soap. He caught it and stood looking at it for a moment, wondering why the others were laughing at him.

"What you goin' do, man?" the prisoner who tossed him the soap asked. "You gonna stare at it all night, or put it to use gettin' some of that funk offa you?"

Tony looked over at his friend, but Gene dropped his eyes.

"You know, man, you don't have to take a bath until you get ready, don't you?" Tony asked.

"It ain't none of your business what he does, my man," one of the men said.

"What's your name, mister?" Tony asked quietly.

"Why?" the short, dark-complexioned man answered.

"I'm just curious," Tony said. "I seem to remember that it was me that came in here with Gene, so I was wondering if some mistake had been made or not."

The short man seemed to gain a little courage from Tony's reply. "They call me Tommy, boy, but before it's over, you might be calling me Daddy Tommy." He laughed sharply.

Tony didn't crack a smile. "Before I do that, mister, one of us will be dead, and I don't mean hurt, I mean dead!"

His threat didn't go unheeded. The ward fell silent, waiting to see what Tommy would do. The long scar on the side of Tommy's face seemed to glow as he broke out in a sweat.

Chester, watching the action, read Tommy quickly. As Tommy glanced around for help, he decided to interfere just to see how much of a coward Tommy was. He could see the fear in the man, as the man glanced around for some of his friends to come to his rescue.

"What's wrong, baby?" Chester asked coldly. "You afraid of a little old peckerwood? One big bad nigger like you? I can't believe my eyes."

"I ain't afraid of no honkie or nigger alive, brother!" the man blustered, trying to show courage where it really wasn't. "You," he said harshly, pointing to Gene, "you gonna take that shower or not?" He had decided to ignore Tony's threat or leave Tony to some of the other brothers. He'd help when they jumped on him, but he'd be damned if he'd be the first one to jump on that young honkie. He had a feeling that the young white boy could fight, and he'd made the mistake before and found out that all white boys weren't afraid of black men.

After glancing at Tony, Gene got up from the table and made his way into the shower. He undressed near the shower, trying to find as much privacy as possible. As soon as the water started to run, the dogs went into action.

Tommy was the first one into the shower after Gene. He undressed at the side, dropping his clothes in a heap. He grinned over his shoulder at the other men, making sure not to catch Tony's eye. He went into the shower, followed closely by one of his friends.

"Wait, man, wait!" Gene screamed from the shower. Then the sound of a slap was heard. There was silence for a brief moment, then a scream was heard. "Oh my god, you're killing me. Please, man, please. It's too big. You're busting me open!"

"Shut up, boy, shut your goddamn mouth or you'll get something stuck in it too." It sounded like Tommy, but Chester couldn't be sure. He gritted his teeth. If there was one thing he hated it was the rape of another man. Chester didn't care if they were black, white, or green, just the idea of raping another man got on his nerves. He pushed the chess pieces in front of him around on the board.

"You want to play a game?" Chester glanced up and saw Tony looking down at him.

"Yeah, man. Come on," Chester said, setting up the pieces. It was something to take his mind off of what was going on in the shower. The action from the shower brought back memories of when he was just a boy, trying to make his way up from the South. He had caught a ride on a boxcar that was already occupied by an older black man. The man had tried to rape Chester later that night, after giving him some wine. It had ended with Chester getting lucky and sticking eight inches of knife in the man's chest. After searching the man's pockets and removing the ten dollars that he had found there, he had then rolled the body to the door of the boxcar and pushed it out. He had been only fourteen then, but it was an experience that he had never forgotten.

"Oh please, that's enough! Please, please. Help, help!" The sound of another slap could be heard, then only the sounds of grunts and moans.

Chester watched the young white boy in front of him. He was a nice looking kid, Italian, with dark hair, a small nose, and lips that a woman would love to

kiss. He was handsome, and to many of the men inside
the county jail, that meant he was open for their
advances. It was thought that, if a man was handsome,
he had to have some woman in him. There was something else about him, though, and Chester noticed it.
The boy was young, about nineteen, and he was also
solid. He stood an even six feet and looked as if he
had played football all his life.

It was something he didn't generally do, but
Chester wanted to know. Tony was just too cool. "You
ain't worried, man. I guess you know you're on the
menu next."

Tony shrugged his shoulders. "I might be, but you
can bet it won't be that easy for them."

The statement wasn't a boast, he was just stating a
fact. The man meant to fight if he had to.

"What's going on over there?" The sound of one
of the men locked down the rock came to them. "You
boys wouldn't be playing a little sex with them sweet
little white girls they put in there this afternoon, would
you?"

One of the older cons sitting at the table playing
bridge spoke up. "Why don't you do your own time,
con, and quit worrying about what's happening down
this way."

"You guys get all the luck. Every time they bring
some white girls in here, they always put them down
there. I think I'm goin' get transferred down there
myself so I can get in on some of that good pussy."

"You might come down here and end up gettin'
fucked yourself, my man," another man at the card

table yelled back. The men burst out laughing—loud, Negro laughter, the sound that could only be made by blacks, spontaneous, universal. Wherever blacks congregate, whether a congenial gathering or not, if humor surfaced, it was a black sound.

"Why don't you guys break that shit up? All you goin' do is bring the dep back here fuckin' with us, and we're supposed to get the TV set sometime this week. You guys'll fuck that up," another prisoner yelled from ward three.

"My man's right," an elderly prisoner they called Pop said. Pop stared around at the younger convicts. "You know Flip Wilson comes on this week, and if we're lucky, we might just get the TV set on that night."

The men fell silent. His words of wisdom made sense, even if they resented someone telling them to be quiet. They looked forward to the one day a week the television set was brought down to their rock. If they were disorderly, the television was withheld from them. It was the one privilege the deputies controlled that could be used against them. The threat of withholding the television set was a strong one. That was the last thing the men wanted to happen.

Tommy was the first man out of the shower. He strutted around with his small chest stuck out as if he had just done something important.

"Man, oh man," he said loudly, "that was sure 'nough pussy." He glanced over at Tony, making sure that what he said was heard. "Yeah, man, that was what I call real penitentiary pussy. That ol' girl is all

right! I'm goin' see to it that she's taken care of." He
walked over to his bunk and fumbled around under
his pillow until he found what he was looking for. He
withdrew a candy bar and flashed it around.

One of his partners came out of the shower and
saw Tommy with the candy. "Hey, Tommy, give me
a piece of the sweetness, man. I'll straighten up with
you when the store comes around."

"You want to sell one of those candy bars,
Tommy?" Willie asked. Tommy shook his head no,
and Willie asked loudly, "Is there anyone in here who
has some candy or a pie or something to sell? I'll buy
it, whatever it is, if it's from the store wagon."

"Hey, blood," a tall slim brother yelled from his
bunk, where he had been reading. "I got some cupcakes I'll sell you, man."

Tommy laughed loudly, "You better believe the
Preacher will sell you something. It will cost you three
times as much as what it cost him from the wagon,
blood."

"The name ain't blood. Call me Willie, man—if
you have to call me anything," Willie said sharply.
Chester glanced up at his new partner. Willie had
some strange ways for a young man. He acted older
than he really was, Chester reflected. Maybe that was
why he liked the young man; he seemed mature for
a kid his age.

Gene finally came out of the shower. Tommy called
him over and put his arm around his shoulders as
though he were a woman. "Here, honey," he said, "I
saved this just for you." He held out the candy bar.

For a brief moment, Gene hesitated, then he took the candy bar. "Thanks," he murmured shyly. He moved slowly, breaking the embrace. His walk was wide legged as if he was hurt. With downcast eyes, he walked over to where Tony and Chester were playing chess. He opened the candy wrapper and shyly offered a piece of the candy to Tony.

"Man, get that shit away from here," Tony said coldly, not taking his eyes away from the chess board. Gene held the candy out towards Chester, who reached over and took a piece.

"Hey, Preach, How much did you say you wanted for that cupcake?" Willie asked.

"Fifty cents, my man, just fifty cents," Preacher said, not bothering to take his eyes from the book he was reading.

"Oh, man, that's too damn much. I can understand you making a profit out of it, but that's three times as much as they cost on the wagon." Willie answered as he dug down in his pockets and examined the loose change he had. "No, baby, I got to buy some cigarettes, so I can't afford that much money for cupcakes. How much would you charge for a pack of smokes, if you had some?"

"Well, it just so happens that I do have some," Preacher answered as he laid his book down and reached under his pillow. He pulled out a carton which held cupcakes and cigarettes. "When is the wagon due back on this rock, Pops?" he asked suddenly.

The old gray-haired man at the card table scratched his head. "I think it should be back on this rock day after tomorrow, if I'm not wrong. But you know how that goes, Preach, you cain't never tell 'bout that fuckin' wagon until it really shows up."

"How much do you want for your cigarettes?" Tony asked quietly. His voice brought on a sudden silence to the prison ward. Chester glanced up from his game of chess. He knew instantly what was wrong. The black prisoners must have been in the habit of taking the money from all the white inmates. That explained why the white boys were picking up the butts and tearing them open and rerolling them. He had noticed it, but as such things go, he hadn't really paid any thought to it, thinking that maybe the white boy he'd seen picking up the butts had just been broke. Now he knew, without a doubt, from the silence that fell on the ward when Tony had spoken up. Now the shit would be in the fan, he thought. Tony had brought it to a head, unwillingly. It was too late to retract his words.

"Boy, you got some money?"

The words came from Larry, a tall brown-skinned Negro who was beginning to turn fat while still in his late twenties. His gut hung over the dirty blue jeans. "You hear me, honkie? I asked you if you had some money," Larry said as he walked around the table so that he stood right behind Tony.

"My cigarettes cost one dollar a pack, man, and I ain't got but three packs left," the Preacher said loudly so that all of the men could hear.

"Goddamn, baby, you sure are high with your stuff," Willie snapped, anger beginning to show in his voice. He shoved the change back into his pocket, not having enough to buy a pack.

"How much were you short, Willie?" Tony asked him quietly, ignoring the man behind him.

Willie shrugged. "That's all right, man, he wants too much for the damn things anyway. I'd rather quit smoking first."

"You ain't got no money no-way, white boy," Larry said. "All that shit you got in your pocket belongs to me. Now set it out before I get mad."

Slowly Tony got up from the table, never glancing at the man behind him. He exploded in motion. Using his elbow, he caught Larry on the jaw with a hard blow, and still turning, he followed it up with a right cross to Larry's chin, then shot a combination of powerful punches into Larry's overripe stomach.

Larry let out a grunt and slumped forward, almost out on his feet, but Tony didn't stop. He knew enough about jailhouse fighting to know that you had to hurt a man when you fought him or quit sleeping at night. In an open bay or ward, where prisoners can walk around at night, it was too dangerous to allow a man you had not fought hard and therefore had not instilled fear into, to be able to tip up on you while you slept.

Tony grabbed the slumping man by his dirty shirt and spun him around, shoving him viciously, head first, into the steel bars. As the man bounced back, he grabbed him by the back of his shirt and pants and pushed him viciously back into the bars again. The steel bars did the rest of his work. The sound of breaking bones could be heard. It had happened so fast,

Larry's dog pack didn't have time to interfere. After seeing what had happened to their partner, the rest of them didn't have the nerve to go to Larry's rescue.

"Dep on two, dep on two," Pops yelled loudly. "We need a doctor back here!"

One of the prisoners in the first ward took up the yell until finally the sound of the outer steel doors being opened was heard.

Tony grabbed Larry's semi-conscious body and pushed it away from where they were playing chess. Larry fell, sprawled face down, by the door.

"What's going on back there?" the night deputy asked from the front of the corridor.

"There's been an accident back here," one of the card players yelled back at the deputy. "You better get a stretcher. A man's been hurt."

The deputy came running back towards the ward. He glanced in at the unconscious man lying on the floor. "What happened to him?" he asked, studying the pool of blood that was beginning to form beneath the man's head.

"He was running to get to the toilet and slipped, I guess. Fell head first into the bars," one of the card players said casually.

"Hey, Bob, you better call for a stretcher," the deputy yelled back to his partner, who stood in the doorway waiting for his partner to check out the disturbance. "I guess you guys know that this will blow your television privilege for this week." He glanced at the impassive faces of the men inside the ward. He knew he'd never get the truth out of them this way.

They'd have to be taken out one at a time, then one of them would tell what happened, but never in front of another prisoner. He couldn't blame them; to be a known informer on a ward was almost a sure way of losing your life quickly.

The deputy was white, and as he studied the faces of the men, he saw Gene. "What's your name, boy?" he asked, seeing the fresh bruises on the young man's face. He frowned. "Come over here. Let me get a better look at you." He watched angrily as Gene walked slowly towards him. The boy could hardly walk. The deputy had a damn good idea of just what had happened in Gene's case. The boy's face was marked up and his eye was already turning a bluish red. "You're new on this ward, aren't you?" he asked, already aware that this was one of the new white boys who had been put on the ward that day before he came on shift. "Where's the other boy that came in with you?"

"I'm right here," Tony answered, not bothering to get up.

"Well, get your ass up here so that I can look at you," the deputy said. He waited for Tony to get up, expecting to see his face all marked up too. He was surprised when the rather handsome young man stopped in front of him. The man didn't have a mark on him anywhere. He wondered if the boy was a queer. If so, that would be the reason why he wasn't marked up. He'd probably take a black dick with happiness, so there wouldn't be any reason for the black bastards to whip him, the deputy thought.

He turned his anger on Gene as he waited for the

stretcher. "Who did that to you?" he asked sharply. "You don't have to worry. I'll get the sonuvabitch out of there right now, and you'll never have to worry about him again." His voice was deadly serious.

Gene hesitated for just a brief moment. He hadn't enjoyed what had happened to him, and he knew if the man stayed in there it would happen again. Tears started to flow down his cheeks. He was frightened; the experience would leave an indelible imprint upon him for life. Visualizing it happening over and over and over again intensified his growing fear. Desperately he stared up at the tall deputy, realizing instantly that the deputy spoke the truth.

Tommy also realized that the young white boy was about to break. His knees shook as he thought about the possibilities of what would happen if he was charged with sodomy. He was fighting a simple larceny charge. The most he would get out of it would be two years, but a sodomy charge could get him up to fifteen years.

He stepped up to the bars. "Aw, man, ain't nothin' wrong with Gene. He was just sparring around with one of the boys and got hit in the eye by mistake. I'll personally see to it that it don't happen again."

The deputy eyed Tommy as though he had just crawled from under a rock. "Boy, if you don't want to see the inside of the hole tonight, you better get the hell away from here!" Tommy started back towards his bunk, but the deputy, noticing the way Gene shied away from Tommy, called him back. As Tommy approached the bars, Gene again shied away from him.

"Boy, if you don't like what happened to you," the deputy said, "you better speak up." The sound of the deputy's partner approaching caused him to stop.

"That's all right," the partner said, "I got a better way, then I'll leave it up to you. You treat your people like we're operating a fuckin' home!" He took out his keys as two other deputies came up to the door. He unlocked the steel door and stood back. "Bring your ass on out of there," he said, pointing Gene out to the other deputies. "I think that boy's been gang raped. I want him taken over to the hospital and examined. Also that one there," he said, pointing to Tony. "I don't think he was raped. He just laid down like a fuckin' whore and gave it up. But I want him examined also. If he's full of cum' the doctors will find it, then we'll lock his pretty ass up with the rest of the queers."

Tony blushed down to his shoelaces. He started to take a punch at the deputy as he walked out of the cell. "You're a lying deputy, and I don't like anybody to brand me a queer," he stated loudly as his anger got the better of his judgment.

"Take it easy, kid," Chester said quietly. "We're the ones who have to live with you, Tony, and we know you're a man. So fuck what a goddamn turnkey thinks."

Astonishment flashed across the deputy's face. He started to say something but changed his mind as he glanced at the two colored deputies that had come back with the stretcher. "What's wrong, boy?" he managed to say anyway. "This young kid here must be your girlfriend. You afraid you might get charged with a little sodomy or something like that?"

Chester laughed in his face. "That's the last thing I'm worried about, deputy. I just hate to see you brand that kid a queer, when he ain't."

"I'll just bet he ain't!" the deputy said, sneering. "You bastards ain't got enough decency to allow a boy like that to come in here and do his own time without being tampered with."

Tony turned on the deputy furiously. "You no-good peckerwood, hillybilly bastard! I just wish I could be locked up with you for about five minutes. I'd show you if I was a queer or not." His anger flashed in his eyes, and he seemed about to explode.

The deputy was basically an honest man. His anger had really sprung from the frustration of his inability to stop the rapes that occurred on his shift. This happened because he worked afternoons, and the majority of the rapes happened then. Also, ninety-five percent of the rape victims were white, which really made the deputy angry. He was southern-born. Even the sight of white women visiting some of the black prisoners on visiting day so angered him that he would always find some reason to take away the prisoners' small privileges. The privation that he inflicted on them was cruel, harsh, unjust. Twenty men, every man on the ward, had to suffer because one black man on the ward happened to have a white woman for a wife. With astonishing cunning, the deputy would come up with some reason to take away their television rights.

At times, when he could get away with it—making sure the other deputy on shift with him didn't realize what was happening—he would make arrangements to take away store privileges for a week. This would cause untold hardship for the men inside the ward. They would have to buy their supply of cigarettes and toothpaste and other necessities from the men on the wards down the hall. Everything cost double. A candy bar that cost ten cents at a store on the streets cost fifteen cents on the prison wagon and, when resold by one prisoner to another, the price would reach thirty cents or more. This was when the store had just left. Later on in the week, when these items became scarce, the price for a candy bar would be raised to fifty cents, and the men paid for it gladly, glad to be able to buy a candy bar or anything to kill the hunger pangs, for hunger was something that stayed with the men in the county jail. But the deputy was an honest man. He wouldn't think of stealing something. If he found a wallet in the street containing money, he would return it, unless there were pictures inside of it showing that the owner was black. If that happened, it was a completely different matter.

The deputy looked at Tony's flushed face. "Okay boy," he said easily, "we'll find out if you're all that much of a man. The doctor will damn sure know. If you haven't been tampered with, I'll personally apologize." He glanced at the other white men inside the ward. All of them had marks on their faces. He shook his head. "I'll damn sure apologize, because you'd be a damn sight better man than I give you credit for."

"Let's get on with it," one of the other deputies said as he lifted his end of the stretcher. Gene and Tony were ushered down the corridor behind the men bearing Larry on the stretcher. The sound of their feet faded away, all that could be heard by the men left in the ward was the sound of doors being unlocked and then closed.

Silence fell on the ward. Men glanced at each other uneasily. The same thought was in each of their minds. Pops finally broke the silence: "Well, Tommy, looks like you can start packing your shit."

"What you mean, old man? Stop talkin' crazy. You ain't makin' no sense," he said, afraid to face the truth.

"What's happening over there?" a man asked from another ward. "Looks like somebody's ass is goin' be up shit creek. What you guys do, gang bang them whiteys?"

"It ain't none of your goddamn business," Tommy yelled back, trying to use anger to cover his fear. "They ain't got no damn witnesses," he said, then glanced around the ward. He looked at Chester and Willie. "You guys ain't seen nothing, understand?" he said harshly.

Willie spoke up before Chester could say anything. "Man, what was that? A threat? Or are you asking us not to say anything? You're in enough trouble now, without overloading your weak ass." Chester laughed at his partner's words. It took some of the heat out of him that Tommy's words had aroused.

"Say, brother, Tommy didn't mean any harm. He was just asking if you gonna stay out of this shit, man, that's all," another one of the rape members said. He glanced around at the white boys left in the ward. "Don't none of you bastards go gettin' any ideas, hear? 'Cause if you do, it's goin' go plenty damn hard for you if something comes out of this shit."

"Aw, man, we ain't got nothing to worry about. They ain't got no witnesses, so where is their case? It's our word against his, and he ain't no better than we is," Tommy said.

"What happened to Larry?" a voice from the ward next door inquired. "He sure looked fucked up when they took him past here."

Pops added his little bit: "He made a mistake fuckin' with a man when he thought he was fuckin' with a punk."

"That whitey ain't shit!" Tommy said, still trying to impress people with his mouth instead of his actions.

"If he was such a punk, Tommy, why didn't you try him by yourself?" Chester asked sharply, hitting a sore spot with Tommy.

Tommy rose to the bait. "Listen, man, ever since you came in here you been tossing your weight around. Now I don't know you and I don't give a fuck about you, you dig?" He glared coldly at Chester, his anger getting the better of him. As he stared into Chester's eyes, he realized he had made a big mistake. He hurried to straighten it out as Chester came out of his seat. He put his hands out in front of him as if he was trying to hold off a big weight.

Slowly Chester regained his temper and lit a cigarette. "Boy, you think you got trouble now, but it ain't nothing compared to what you goin' have if you step out of line with me. Now I'm goin' tell you one time and I'm not goin' bother to repeat myself. You ain't goin' be with us too much longer, but for the short time that you're around me, I want total respect from you. Not halfway, but complete respect. The same respect I give every man I meet that shows he's a man."

Seeing that Chester wasn't about to fight, Tommy spoke up. "Well, you ain't been givin' me no hell-u-fied respect since you been in here."

"I said I give respect to those who show that they're men. From what I've seen of you, boy, you're more of an animal than a man, so you don't deserve any respect. What you really deserve is to be offed. You went in there and raped that kid, now you're out here shittin' on yourself, and you think somebody going to respect you?" Chester laughed harshly.

"Wait a minute, brother. If he wasn't no honkie, I wouldn't have bothered him—you understand? No matter how young or weak he was, I wouldn't have fucked with him," Tommy said, and as he saw the disbelief on Chester's face, he added, "I'm for real about that, brother. Ask any of the guys in here. I don't fuck with no brother. If he's already a punk, then that's another matter." They talked over the white boy's heads, not bothering to try and hide what they were saying. It was something that had happened over a hundred years ago, when the white men used to talk in front of their slaves, not bothering to conceal what

they said, because they didn't give the slave the credit of having enough sense to understand what was
being said, or rather, they just didn't give a damn.

"Okay, brother, I can believe that, but I just don't
go along with rape, that's all," Chester replied.

"These white whores like it, my man. They really
do. Come here, Mike," he ordered. As the white boy
got up off the floor where he had been lying, pretending that he had been asleep, Tommy put his arm
around the boy and stuck his other hand down in the
back of the man's pants.

The white boy turned a bright red but stood there
as Tommy played with his ass. Tommy reached down
and pulled out his penis. "Kiss it, Mike. Kiss it the
way I like you to do it."

Mike was short, but he was still an inch or two
taller than Tommy. He shook his head, not wanting to
do it in front of the other men. Quickly Tommy
reached up and caught him by the neck and shook him
roughly. "What did I tell you to do, *bitch*? You done
got to be hard of hearing all at once?" he snarled, and
his voice carried an edge of danger in it that Mike
recognized.

"No, Tommy, you know it's not anything like that.
I just don't like to do things in front of people, you
know. How about putting the blanket down over your
bunk. We can get George to look out for us."

"Bitch, when I need George to look out for me, I'll
ask him. Now get busy doing what I asked you to
do!"

As the young white boy went down on his knees,

Chester shook his head at Tommy's stupidity. The man was in enough trouble already, now the fool was doing just what he shouldn't have been doing. Before, when he had said that there were no witnesses, he had made a point. It wasn't much, but it was a case that he had a chance of fighting. But now, with a ward full of men watching, he was ruining himself. Now there would be more than enough witnesses, if the white boy should get up enough courage to press charges. And Chester believed that, in the morning, everybody in the ward would be questioned, one at a time, and he was equally certain that what Tommy was making Mike do now would also be brought out.

"Oh, God, that's it, white lady, that's it! Hold it right there," Tommy said, still trying to impress the onlookers. "Oh Jesus, goddamn, this is the best head in the goddamn world. I'd give up my front seat in hell for this cap. Oh," he moaned, really feeling it now, "don't let a drop get away, motherfucker." He held the white boy's head tightly with both hands.

Mike tried to pull back, but Tommy had too hard a hold on his head. Tears of frustration ran down Mike's cheeks as the black man held his head and began to come in his mouth. The boy choked on the long black penis in his mouth, but Tommy continued to hold his head tightly. Cum ran from Mike's mouth and down the side of his chin. He choked and gagged, but it didn't do any good. Tommy held on for dear life.

Chester looked away. The rest of the men watched for different reasons. Chester caught the eye of one white boy; the boy was staring daggers at Tommy. If he'd had a gun, he'd have shot Tommy dead in his tracks. That's one more witness against you, Tommy my boy, Chester thought to himself.

When they finished, Tommy wiped his penis off on the white boy's shirt. "There, bitch, if you get hungry tonight, there's some joy juice for you to lick on." He laughed loudly at his own joke, then glanced at the old man, who wasn't smiling. "What's wrong, Pops? You got a love for these funky ass white punks?" he asked harshly.

"No, boy, I ain't got no love for them, but I believe I can stomach them more than I can a nigger like you. And when I use the word *nigger* in your case, it means just what it implies."

"That's true to form, Pops. You old Uncle-Tom-ass niggers are always worrying about whitey, but you can damn well bet whitey ain't worrying about you." Tommy lit a cigarette and blew out the smoke. "I'm goin' make these honkies pay for the three hundred years of sorrow they caused us." He directed his words more at Chester and the old man than at anyone else in the ward.

"Who you trying to bullshit, man?" Chester demanded. "You ain't got to worry about making them pay, because everything you've did to them tonight and other nights, you goin' have to face the grim reaper for." Chester paused, then added, "Don't fool yourself, Tommy; I don't know what you're in here for, but you're more than likely goin' to end up with a sodomy charge sometime tomorrow."

Tommy laughed harshly. "Ain't no witnesses, man. It's my word against Gene's, so he ain't got no case."

Now it was Chester's turn to laugh, and he did it to the limit. He laughed so long and so hard that Tommy demanded, "What's so funny? You don't believe it, huh? You think they can railroad me just because they find some cum in that 'wood's ass?"

"You don't even have to worry about Gene no more, man," Chester replied. "Just look around you. They goin' be over here in the morning, the detectives from across the street, taking guys out of this ward and talking to them one at a fuckin' time, and you can bet on it happening."

"Bullshit!" Tommy exclaimed loudly. "You don't know, man, you're just blowing hot-ass air." He glanced around for assurance. "This cat don't know what the fuck he's talkin' about. If he knew so goddamn much, he sure wouldn't have his ass locked up in here with us."

Chester grinned. "There's something else, too, Tommy. Like I said, you ain't got to worry about Gene no more. They got all the witnesses they need right here in this ward—thanks to the freak show you put on for us." His laughter rang out loud and clear again. Even later on that night, after everyone had turned in, Tommy lay awake, still hearing the sarcastic laughter ringing in his ears.

5

THE SOUND OF THE coffee man coming caused the men lying on the floors and in the tiny bunks to turn out. Chester remained in bed, smoking. He hadn't slept well because of the lights. They had burned all night long, so he was thankful for having gotten the bottom bunk. The bunk on top of him with Willie in it blocked out some of the light, but he knew from past experience that it would just take time to get used to it.

There was also another minor problem he'd have to get used to. Down the rock, in ward four, there were inmates who must have thought that they were the Temptations, because they had sat up most of the

night singing. Whenever someone yelled down to
them to shut up, all they would do was yell back, "Do
your own time." Chester would have bet his last dollar that the singers were now busy snoring. Some men
did their time like that. Since the lights stayed on, you
couldn't really tell day from night.

The two trusties pushing the coffee wagon came
into view and stopped in front of cell-block two, waiting for the turnkey to come up and unlock the door.
The men began to line up like well-trained cows.
When the guard came up and unlocked the door, one
of the trusties pushed a large bucket of jet black,
steaming coffee into the cell.

Pops picked up the bucket and carried it over to
the dinner table. The other trusty began to pass out
an empty cup and a dry breakfast roll through the bars
to each man in line after the deputy had closed the
steel door.

Chester shook Willie awake. "Man, how can you
sleep through all this confusion and noise? If you want
some coffee or a dry roll, you better roll out of that
bunk, 'cause the line is getting shorter."

"Thanks, baby," Willie said, leaping from the bunk.
Chester followed him towards the rear of the line.
"Maybe we can get lucky and bum some sugar to go
with that strong-ass coffee," Chester said as they fell
in on the rear of the line.

"Well now," Preacher said, overhearing them. "I
guess you boys are pretty lucky. I just happen to have
a box of sugar that hasn't been opened yet. I'll let it
go to you fellows for a good price."

"How much?" Willie asked sharply, remembering the steep prices the man had quoted the day before.

"Well now, since you guys seem to be all right, I'll give you a deal. I paid thirty-five cents for it on the wagon, so I'll give it to you for just fifty cents. Is that a deal or not?"

"I'll handle it, Willie," Chester said quietly, not wanting to embarrass his new friend, who he believed was almost broke. After receiving their coffee and stale roll, they followed Preacher back to his bunk, which he had never taken his eyes from while in the line.

Chester wondered idly how the man guarded his goods when taking a shower. "Give us a package of them cupcakes and also a couple packs of those cigarettes. We better prepare for it in case the wagon don't make it up this way this week."

"Of course, of course," Preacher said quickly. "It's just possible that we have lost our store privilege for the week because of what happened last night."

After paying the man for the stuff, Chester tossed a pack of cigarettes to Willie, who put up a weak protest. "Don't worry about it, Willie. If you want to, you can repay me whenever you get a visit." He opened up the cupcakes and held one out to Willie.

"No, man, no. That stuff cost too much money for you to share the cupcake with me too. I appreciate the smokes, baby, I mean I really do."

Reluctantly Chester drew back the offer. He knew the man's pride was riding him. He realized that he should have bought two packs of cupcakes; that way,

Willie probably would have accepted. "Your misguided pride will sure make you go hungry in here,
Willie, unless you get it together." Before Willie could
say anything, Chester continued, "If we're going to
be partners, man, we have to share and share alike."

"Okay, Chester, my man. I'll tell you what we'll
do. Since you've got the cupcakes and we're partners,
how about settin' out the roll?"

"Well, I'll be damned," Chester exclaimed. "I was
debating tossing this fuckin' thing in the shitter, man,
now you make me shame. I can't eat this cupcake
while you break your teeth on this hard-ass roll."

"Don't worry about it," Willie answered as he
poured sugar into his coffee. He held up his roll,
which was almost gone. "See, I don't have no trouble getting them down."

Chester shrugged and handed over the roll. "I wonder what time the shit is goin' start," he said. "I see
they didn't bring Tony and them back last night. I can
understand them holding Gene at the hospital, but why
would they keep Tony?"

Willie didn't have an answer for the question. "You
seem to be pretty sure they're coming over here and
hassle us today, ain't you?"

"You can bet on it, Willie. It probably won't jump
off until around ten o'clock. The detectives didn't generally get off their asses until that time. They'll have
their coffee break, then shoot the shit for a while; after
that, they'll have a nice long talk with Gene, then the
shit will begin."

"I don't know, man," Willie said, shaking his head.

"Gene was in the shower, plus the dudes made him wash up when he finished, so there probably won't be any traces of the shit left in him."

"Don't fool yourself on that, blood. After taking that many dicks, there's going to be more than enough traces for them to go on. Also, the fact the boy walked as if he had been busted open. Didn't you notice how wide legged he walked?"

"Yeah, I did notice that. I don't see how anybody could miss that fact. You're probably right, though. Sometime around ten or ten thirty we'll get a visit from the boys in blue."

They finished their breakfast in silence, then took their cups back up to the front of the cell and set them down. Neither man wanted any more of the extra strong tasting coffee.

* * *

The morning passed slowly. The card players took up their positions at the table and began their endless routine of card playing. Chess boards were brought out, and the men who could play began their steady playing, which would last until evening, broken up only by the coming and going of the dinner wagon.

As the morning wore on, Tommy regained some of his lost confidence. "Well, big fellow, looks like you didn't know what the fuck you were talkin' about after all. It's past ten o'clock, and ain't nothing jumped off yet." His laughter rang out, releasing some of the terrifying fear that seemed to almost overwhelm him. He had slept with it, tasting it in his mouth, feeling it deep down in his gut, and now the premonition of trouble was leaving. Tommy could relax—or so he thought.

The sound of the outer doors opening brought all of the men alert. They could hear the footsteps of many men coming down the corridor. It was too early for the deputies to be bringing new prisoners up, so it had to be something else. Everything in the county jail went on a steady routine; any change brought instant alertness. They knew when the deputies were expected to make their rounds, when the lawyers came up to visit the various men, and even when the doctor was making his so-called rounds—which was rare indeed.

Voices drifted down the rock to the waiting men. This was it. There was no doubt left. There were too many voices out there for it to be anything different. Chester had been right after all. Before any other possibilities could be kicked back and forth between the waiting men, they were there: two white detectives and four deputies.

"Ron Jacoby, Mike Francois, front and center!" the deputy with sergeant stripes on his arm yelled. The two white men stepped forward and stood at the door waiting for it to open. Another one of the deputies took out his keys and opened the door.

To the waiting men, this revealed to them just how serious it was. They weren't bothering with throwing the lock from the master control. It was seldom that a turnkey opened the door with his key. Always, the deputy standing up front threw the lock from the master control—except on those occasions when the goon squad came back to quiet down a troublemaker. Then they didn't bother with the slow process of waiting until the doors were opened from up front either.

The two detectives glared into the ward at the black men huddled around the card table. "You boys better finish up your game; it might be awhile before some of you are able to play again," one of the detectives said coldly as he turned to leave.

Perspiration broke out on Tommy's forehead. "Man," he said loudly to no one in particular, "you think that punk, Mike, will say something?"

His partners in the gang-rape gathered around him. Blue, tall, skinny, and jet black with yellow, rotting teeth, spoke sharply: "If you hadn't made that punk suck your dick last night, we probably wouldn't have no trouble this morning!"

"Goddamn, Blue, you don't believe that shit do you? Don't forget, they had already took that bitch, Gene, out of here, so what I did to Mike don't mean nothing," Tommy replied impatiently.

Danny, a medium-sized man who had been a dope fiend on the street, spoke up: "Tommy's right about one thing, though; it don't mean a thing to us about what he did to Mike last night. It wasn't none of us involved; it's Tommy's little baby, all by his self."

"You motherfuckin' chicken-shit bastard, you!" Tommy cursed. "I should have known you mother-fuckers would end up trying to shift all the weight on me." His voice carried a humble note in it, a sound that hadn't been there earlier. The callousness he had shown the white men was gone; now he wanted pity.

The sight of Tommy starting to break before he even talked to the detectives filled Chester with disgust. The other two white men, George and John Romario, watched silently from their mattresses on the floor. They had pulled the mattresses as far back out of the way as possible. Both men had marks on their faces, too. Chester knew without asking that they had both been raped—probably numerous times—since they'd been on the ward.

The sound of the door opening put the men back on alert. Two deputies came down the corridor. This time, before they even reached ward two, the door began to open. "George Wade, John Romario. Get your asses front and center," one of the deputies yelled.

As the men got up to leave, Chester didn't miss the cold smile on Romario's face. It had been Romario who had stared so hard at Tommy when Tommy had forced Mike to perform fellatio on him.

"Yeah, Tommy boy," Chester said callously, "looks like it's your turn to get the shitty end of the stick. When those detectives get finished interviewing them peckerwoods, they goin' to be some mad white men!"

"If I was you, Tommy," Pops said, "I'd be stickin' some books down inside the back of my pants or something, 'cause them honkies is goin' kick you dead in your black ass."

"Don't go gettin' smart, old man," Tommy growled. "It ain't too late for me to kick you in your black ass before I leave!" Even though he'd made the threat, there was such a look of anguish on his face that a person could tell his mind wasn't on what he was really saying. The man was scared; his eyes were starting to roll, and his body jerked uncontrollably.

Well I'll be damned, Chester said to himself. The man was really a coward after all. There was no pity in his heart for the man, because the way Chester looked at it, there was no excuse for the crime the man had committed. To rape another man was just about one of the lowest things a man could stoop to, he reasoned.

"I wonder why they didn't take nobody out of here but the white boys?" Danny asked suddenly. "It don't seem right. If they was going to go about this right, seems as if they'd try talking to some of the brothers in here and get both sides of the goddamn story."

Preacher laid his book aside for a brief moment. "How you young black boys fool yourselfs is beyond me," he said. "You should have realized that what you've been doing would finally catch up with you. You, Danny, you're being held for armed robbery, so it shouldn't make any difference to you. I thought that was the reason why you just didn't care. You knew that when they caught you, they couldn't give you any more time than what you're going to get anyway."

As Danny grinned, Preacher continued. "The only fool in the bunch was Tommy. Robert, he's fighting a murder case, so it doesn't make him any difference either. But Tommy, our smart friend there, he's the only one in here that I know of who hasn't got anything to keep him awake at night. Or should I have said, didn't *have* anything to keep him awake until now.

"Any black man with any knowledge whatsoever
is aware of the facade of democracy and freedom and
justice for all our courtrooms are known for. This poisonous pus of double-standard justice, this racial bigotry that so overflows in our courtrooms is a known
fact. A black man is guilty until he can prove different, and then, sometimes when he has proven it to be
different, he is still found guilty because of his black
skin. So why would you fool yourself and think these
detectives would be any different?" With a snort, the
Preacher picked up his book and continued reading as
if he had never been interrupted.

Chester stared at the man in astonishment. There
was a personality there that he knew was definitely
different from the run-of-the-mill individuals that one
ran into while in the county jail.

Suddenly the corridor doors banged open. Before
the guards reached the cellblock, the door began to
open. Chester spoke quietly to Willie, "This is it, baby,
I'll bet you a smoke on it."

Before Willie could reply, four of the deputies stood
in front of the cell; none of the men were smiling.
"When I call your names, I want you niggers to gath-
er your stuff and bring it with you, 'cause you won't
be coming back." The sergeant said loudly, anger
showing in his every move. "Danny Tomson, Robert
Danials, Marcus...." He glanced at a small piece of
paper in his hand, then added, "Marcus Blue Lanford,
Tommy Johnson. You boys got one minute, then we're
coming in after you."

The men quickly gathered up their belongings. As they walked out of the cell, Tommy tried to show an air of confidence. He twisted around and started to speak, "I'll see...."

That was as far as he got. The sergeant kicked him in the butt as hard as he possibly could. "Nigger," the sergeant growled, "when I tell you to move, I mean just that! You ain't got time to visit. Now get a move on or you'll get another taste of that!"

Tommy moved, holding his backside as his face twisted up as if he was about to cry. Before the door closed, Tony came in by himself.

The work-hardened sergeant waited until the door was closed, then said, "I want you niggers to know I ain't going to tolerate no shit like what's been happening in here. Now them boys we just took out are going to the hole, and they'll be there for a while. After they come out of there, we got a special ward on the old side that we don't put anyone in except men involved with rape or sodomy." He glared at the men inside the cage, then added, "If that ain't enough, keep this in mind. These boys are all going over to court sometime this week because charges of sodomy are being brought against them, so they'll have another case to fight besides the ones they're already here on."

He started to walk away, then stopped, "I'm not going to take your store privileges away this time, because we have all the men who have been involved in this mess. But if this ward gives me any more trouble, it will be a cold day in hell before you see the store on this rock again."

Another deputy came hurrying up, clutching a piece of paper. He whispered hurriedly into the sergeant's ear. "Break four, damnit," the sergeant roared, then led the way on down the rock. In a couple of minutes he was back, herding the two men who had been taken out of the ward the day before. Both men were complaining as they walked past, carrying their small bundles of personal belongings.

The men inside the ward glanced at each other.

"What's happening out there, Tony?" Chester said.

Tony shook his hand. "I don't really know. When I got off the elevator they had them sitting around the desk, except one, who I guess was talking to some guy who looked like a detective. Then they took Gene off the elevator and rushed him into one of those small offices. The turnkey brought me on back over here. We talked to the detectives this morning, but since nothing happened to me, they weren't interested in what I had to say." He laughed, then sat down at the table. "We must have been important, though. We didn't have to wait downstairs until the dinner wagon came, anyway."

"That's a sure'nuff fact," Chester replied, then both men laughed. Tony grinned; he knew he had been accepted on the ward. His living conditions would be a hell of a lot easier because of that small fact.

6

THE DAYS PASSED slowly into weeks, the weeks slower yet into months, until Chester could count in days the time he had to go before he appeared in court. Willie had been over and had been found guilty of armed robbery. Now he was waiting for his sentence day.

Chester lay back on his bunk and closed his eyes. He had noticed Tony glancing over in his direction, but he didn't feel up to their morning game of chess, so he pretended to be still taking a nap. They had gotten to be pretty close, Tony, Willie, and Chester. They ate their meals together, played cards together, and everything else that could be done in such a small space. The ward hadn't changed much; all but two of the original white men had left, being replaced by three others. The new brothers that came on the ward quickly learned that Tony was the one white man on the ward who kept his own stuff. Every now and then, one of the other white men would be pressured by one of the new blacks, but Pops made it a point to inform him of what had happened to the other brothers. Each of them had been taken to court and made an example of. Each man had been given seven and a half to fifteen years. The newspapers had played it up, so the justice department had gone to work quickly, giving the men involved extreme punishment and hoping that it would work to put fear in the hearts of other inmates.

Chester counted up the months he had been confined. Two weeks away from six months, he thought. At least he had half a year in on his prison sentence, but the way he felt, he'd rather do two years in prison than one in the county jail. He slowly drifted off into a mind-relaxing sleep.

*   *   *

The boat rocked slowly back and forth as he tossed his line overboard again. So far he had caught three fish, but as far as he was concerned, he didn't have to catch another one for the rest of the year. His wife, Marie, was the one who loved fishing so much. He watched the heavyset woman sitting in the front of the rowboat. She was contented as she tossed her line back in She squealed with joy whenever she thought she had a catch on the end of it.

"Oh my, honey, I believe I got a big one this time," she screamed, as Chester watched, silently hoping that she would turn over the boat.

For the tenth time he glanced at the shore. They were on a small creek, but the man who rented out the boats had warned him that the creek was deep, about twenty feet in some spots. He didn't mind, though. He could have swum back and forth between the two shores fifty times without getting tired. On the farm where he was born, they swam in the creek behind the house every day. He and his brother had raced up and down in the muddy water, fearing only the occasional water moccasins that also liked to swim in the creek. How he wished for a water moccasin now. It would have been the answer to his problem. All he'd have had to do was put the damn snake under the seat of the boat; she'd eventually step on the snake, or it would get tired of staying in the shade and come out on its own.

It was a beautiful thought, Chester reasoned, but since he didn't have a snake, he'd just have to make out the best he could. The only other thing he could come up with was flipping the boat over, and that was going to be a job with her sitting right up front, noticing everything that went on. Chester reached under his seat and pulled out the fifth of whiskey he kept there.

"Honey, now honey, don't drink so much of that nasty stuff! It's not even seven o'clock in the morning yet, and you're spilling that rotgut. It's not good for you. I really can't understand why you use it.

Please honey, please, for me, dear." Marie talked on and on; her voice rubbed his already raw nerves until he felt like strangling her to make her shut up.

Goddamn it, goddamn it, goddamn it! he murmured over and over. I'll kill the fuckin' bitch. I'll kill her! "Shut up, bitch, *s*hut up!" he screamed, then he awoke and found himself sitting up in bed, covered with sweat.

*   *   *

Willie was standing over him, with Tony standing just behind Willie. Both men looked concerned. "You all right, baby? You got yourself together?" Willie asked.

Slowly Chester got himself under control. "Was I rappin' in my sleep, blood?" he asked quietly, not wanting to show his concern. But he realized at once what he had been dreaming about. It wasn't the first time it had happened, but before, he had been with his wife, and she knew about it. She had even helped plan it—to a degree.

It had been just as much of Irene's idea to drown Marie as it had been Chester's. Normally he didn't do anything with anyone. In this case he had carried it out alone, too. But Irene had mentioned it to him, that it would be a good way to get rid of a wife if someone was tired of one. She hadn't brought out any names, she had just mentioned it. She also mentioned the number of people who drowned every year up at the resort. They'd get full of whiskey, then go fishing, and sooner or later one of them would turn over the flimsy boats they rented. Half of them weren't even aware that the water was as deep as it was. But now, the man who rented the boats made it a point to inform all the people.

"No, baby, you didn't say nothing. You were just yelling for everybody to shut up. That's when I looked over at you and realized that you were really asleep. Man, you can sure holler in your sleep," Willie said, making it sound like a joke.

Chester examined Willie's face, trying to determine if his buddy was holding back anything. He decided that Willie was telling the truth. There was no reason for him to lie about something like this. He didn't have the slightest idea what it was about, so why would he lie?

"Hey, man," Chester yelled at Tony, breaking the silence that fell between them, "why don't you brew up some of that fine tea you make so well, huh?"

"Fuck that shit, man," Tony replied. "Who was your slave last month this time, huh?" he asked as he walked around to his bunk, which was right next to Chester's. He pulled out the tea bags.

"Let me see, let me see. Last month this time I believe it was you or Willie, Tony my boy. Don't forget, both of you jive-ass motherfuckers are so far in my debt—thanks to the brilliance of my chess playing—that I shall have two dedicated slaves until the end of my bit. In other words, until this small vacation on the state is completed." Chester laughed to take the sting out of his words and show that he was just joking, then added, "If you fix the tea just right, I might just break down and pull out some cupcakes to go with it."

"Hey, Chester oh man, how about settin' out a piece
of that cupcake this way?" a young brother who had
been on the ward for about a month asked. Ever since
Sonny had arrived, he had been begging either cigarettes or food. When his visitors left him any money,
he'd spend it on candy and cupcakes, then bum cigarettes the rest of the week. Sometimes he'd buy one
pack but never any more. At times he'd sell the pork
off his tray because he swore he didn't eat pork, so
he did manage to get a pack whenever they served
pork chops or something that one of the men thought
was worth a pack of cigarettes.

Chester didn't say anything; he just broke off a
piece of the cupcake and held it out to the man. Sonny
stood around in the background and watched the men
have their small party. He gritted his teeth when he
saw Chester give Tony a whole cupcake, but he didn't
say anything. The morning slipped away, replaced by
the afternoon. The card game went on. Chester and
his group sat on his bed, chatting and playing dirty
hearts.

Right before dinner time, they brought back the
men who had gone to court that morning. Preacher
and Pops both had had their day in court. They came
in carrying their trays of food. "What they serving
today?" was the question that hit them as soon as they
entered the ward. The men were too polite to ask how
they came out in court. It was one of the questions
you left up to the other man to state. If he wanted to
tell you, he would. If not, it was none of your busi-

ness.

Pops slammed his bowl down. "I got to go back over tomorrow. The jury ain't made up their minds yet. I still got a chance to win it, I hope." He scooped up a spoon of beans and let it fall back to the bowl. The men glanced over his shoulder to see what was being served. Whatever he had in his bowl, was what they would get on the wagon whenever the trusties brought up their food. "Beans, with small pieces of pork floating around in them," Pop informed the men who hadn't seen his food.

"Goddamn it," Sonny swore. "They fuck up everything with that goddamn pork! Can't they serve something without they have to put pig in it? Even when they have potatoes, they have fuckin' pork mixed up in it!"

"Well, you ain't got to worry about it, boy. Scarce as the meat is in this shit, don't worry about eating no pig. It just ain't there even if you look for it. I just happened to run across a piece, that's all."

Sonny stared at the bowl of food Preacher had put down on the bed. "What's wrong, man? Don't you want your food?" he inquired.

"Don't bother him!" Pops ordered sharply. "He went for sentence today, man. Can't you see the man got something on his mind?"

Sonny looked at the man. No, he couldn't tell, because Preacher was doing what he always did, except this time he wasn't reading a book, he was just lying on his bunk staring upward. "What's wrong, man, the judge toss the book at you or something?"

Sonny asked, breaking the tacit agreement the men had on the ward.

Preacher turned over and stared at the boy. "Yes, I would guess you could call it something like that, kid. Since it is customary for our justice department to handle the uncontrollable crime problem here in our city, the honorable judge felt in his differential application of justice that it would be detrimental if I were to ever join society again, so he sentenced me accordingly."

"What? What?" Sonny stuttered, not really understanding what Preacher had said.

Chester had understood the man though, but he couldn't believe what he had heard. He knew Preacher had killed his wife and the man he had found in his bed with his wife, but that wasn't premeditated murder.

"Preacher, I don't mean no harm, man, but you don't mean they gave you life, do you?" Chester asked, shocked to his toes. He had a built-in horror of life in prison, dating back to the first time he had gone there when he was just eighteen. The very thought of life behind bars filled him with a cold fear that made him feel as if his very bones were shaking.

All of the men waited for Preacher to answer the question. "No, Chester, I don't mean they gave me life, natural life. I think in our state that means I'll never be allowed to make parole." With that, he rolled over and closed his eyes, informing everybody by his actions that he didn't want to be bothered.

"How about lettin' me have that bowl of beans,

man, if you ain't goin' eat it?" Sonny asked loudly, invading the man's thoughts.

Without saying a word, the Preacher got up from his bunk, picked up the bowl of beans, walked over to the toilet and dumped the food into it. He returned to his bunk, still without speaking, and lay back down.

"Well I'll be a motherfucker," Sonny said, his anger rising. "Did you see that shit?" he asked to no one in particular.

"Yeah, I saw it," Willie said hotly. "And if you don't shut your goddamn mouth, I'm going to find out if I'm able to close it for you." He glared at Sonny. The way his eyes were flashing, it could be seen that he wasn't pretending.

Sonny's voice became high-pitched: "Man, I don't know what's wrong with you guys on this rock. I mean, I ain't never run into no shit like this!"

Pops interfered before it went any further. "Boy, I don't know what's wrong with you, but you better learn how to shut up your fuckin' mouth. These men ain't playin' with you, can't you see that? Your mama ain't had no complete fool, did she?"

For some reason it finally dawned on him that he was treading on thin ice. Preacher was lying on his bunk, staring at nothing, and Willie stood at the foot of Chester's bunk glaring at him. He caught the message and shut his mouth.

Later, when the food wagon came, the men sat around eating in silence. Sonny ran back and forth between the men trying to sell his bowl. "I'll let it go for just one pack of cigarettes," he said. When he didn't get any buyers, he lowered his price. "How about a candy bar then? One small ten-cent candy bar." He still didn't find any buyers, so he went to the front of the bars and called out, "Hey, you guys in ward one or three. I'm selling a bowl of beans for just a candy bar. Anybody over there interested?"

"It's a guy over here in three who says he'll give you three cigarettes for it, blood," came the answer. After waiting a few minutes, Sonny started working the bowl down the bars. He had to start at the front door and handle it hand-over-hand because that was the only place large enough to get the bowl out of. "Hey, brother," he called as he worked, "ya goin' have to send me an empty bowl so that when they take the count over here, the bowls won't come up short."

"Don't worry about it," the man said as he held out the cigarettes. As he talked, another man was already sliding an empty bowl down the catwalk.

As Sonny returned to the dinner table and lit up one of the cigarettes, Preacher got up from his bunk and used the toilet. When he turned away from the stool, he stopped and spoke to Sonny. "Listen, boy, I'm not going to repeat myself, so listen close. As long as I'm here, and I've been on this small rock for one year and six months—with two weeks added in—no matter how long I remain here before they send me to prison, do me and yourself a favor. Don't bother to speak to me about anything. Do I make myself clear? I don't want to threaten you, but I do want you to pay heed to what I'm saying. Don't you get in my face no more, as long as we're here, 'cause if you do,

I'll kill you!"

There was no signifying, because every man, including Sonny, knew that it was no idle threat. Death walked among them on that small ward, just as close as it walks wherever violent men are incarcerated.

7

THE MORNING STARTED as usual; the sound of the coffee wagon caused the late sleepers to roll out if they wanted to get their breakfast.

"What they got on the menu this morning, captain?" Willie asked sleepily from his bed.

"That's all right, young blood," Chester replied. "You just stay in bed. I'll get your box of cereal for you. I think we're having cornflakes this morning, but ain't no sense in gettin' up for that tiny little old box. They don't pass out but one box to a man, so why bother?"

Before Chester had finished talking, Willie had hit the floor. On the mornings that they passed out corn-

flakes, everyone either got out of bed or missed out
on their small container of milk. Some of the men in
the front of the line tried to steal an extra carton of
milk, because there was almost always someone who
would rather sleep than get out of bed for cornflakes
and milk. Sometimes, with the right guard on, the men
were able to beg two or three extra boxes of cereal,
and these were then split up among the men who were
in front of the line.

Tony fell in line beside them. "Well, this is my
morning of truth," he said casually, meaning that he
was due in court that morning to fight his armed-rob-
bery charge. Tony would have been out on bond, but
a man had been shot during the robbery, so his bond
had been set extra high—twenty-five thousand dollars.

"There's going to be one busy courtroom this morning, ain't it?" Willie added. He had been going across
the street for the past three days fighting his case.

"It must make you guys feel important being able
to go out every day and leave me sitting up here all
alone," Chester said, wishing quietly that he could go
across the street with them, just to get out of the ward.
A change of scenery would be just fine, he thought.

"Don't sound so sad," Willie warned him. "You'll
be on your way to court next week, so it will be our
turn to wait patiently for you to return."

"With that attitude, you must not be thinking of
beating your case, Willie," Chester said, signifying.

Tony laughed. "I told you that you might as well
go on and plead guilty, since you like it here so much.

You don't want to leave us," he said, nudging Willie in the side with his elbow.

Willie pointed ahead of them at Sonny, who was taking two milks. That meant that someone would go without, unless he was sleeping, then his milk was fair game for whoever took it, unless he had a friend pick it up for him to hold until he woke up. But as it was, no one was in the bed. Everyone in the ward had gotten in line so that they could get their cereal.

After checking the beds, Willie and Tony glanced behind them, only to find out that they were the last ones in line. "Well," Tony said, "looks like it's my milk he took, since I'm the one on the end of the line." He bit on his bottom lip.

When they got to the door, there was cereal for everyone, but the wagon man was short one carton of milk. Tony didn't bother to argue with the man about another carton of milk. He walked slowly over to where Sonny was sitting. "Say, my man," he began, "the wagon ran out of milk, so you'll have to kick back the extra milk you took."

"Man, I don't know what you're talking about. I ain't took nothing but what I had coming," Sonny answered sharply. He stared up at Tony, sneering, "I'm sorry about that, kid."

"You're telling a motherfuckin' lie!" Willie said. "We saw you take the milk, man, so set it out. If you had got away with it, that would have been cool, man, but you got busted. So ain't nothing to do but make it right."

"Hey, baby, what's your problem? I see you got

your milk in your hand, so what's the motherfuckin' trouble?" He stood up, anger showing in his face.

Before he could react, Chester walked up to the bunk from the other side, reached down, picked up his bowl of cereal and milk, reached under his pillow and got the extra carton of milk, and grinned. "Well then, I guess this belongs to whoever finds it," he said coolly, as he walked back towards his bunk.

"Hey, man, what the fuck's going on? That's my cereal you got in your hands, man," Sonny said, trying to get around the bunk.

Willie put his hand on Sonny's chest and shoved him back down on his bunk. "Ain't none of that shit yours, blood! You just made a mistake, that's all." He turned his back and joined Chester at their bunk. When Tony walked up, Chester tossed him his milk.

As soon as Sonny got up the nerve to come over to their bunk, he came up yelling. "Hey, man, ain't nobody goin' buy that shit ya workin' out of. What the fuck you take me for, anyway?"

No one answered him. The men continued to split up the small box of cereal as he watched. They poured milk on his breakfast and began to eat, as he stood there watching them helplessly.

As the other men became aware of what was happening, they set up a raucous, high-pitched cacophony of sound, each man roaring as if it was the funniest thing in the world. It made the old men in the ward happy, because on many a morning their food had come up missing and they had known who had taken it, but Sonny would never give it back up. At last,

seeing the shoe on the other foot made them happy.
They hoped silently that it would bring an end to the
stealing of trays, because there was never enough food
for anyone, let alone enough to allow someone to lose
a meal. Glancing over their cups of coffee, they
watched in silence, wondering what would happen
next. Now they would find out if Sonny was as tough
as he had made out. They knew that he would put up
some kind of fight—or at least hoped that he would.
It would break the boredom, something different, definitely something out of the ordinary.

"I don't know what you guys expect, but I ain't
buying this shit," Sonny stated as he watched them
begin to eat his food. "Hell no! Ain't no way for me
to accept this shit!" The longer he talked, the more
angry he became. His voice rose almost to a scream.
"Goddamn it! Somebody is going to pay me for my
shit!" He glared at Chester, then decided he'd better
find someone easier to lean on.

"Man," Tony said, "you know, in the streets this is
something I'd never eat. My mother always served
eggs for breakfast. I mean no matter what day, it's
always eggs—fried eggs at that. I got so sick of eating eggs seven days a week that I went out and bought
some of them frozen pancakes. You know the kind I
mean? All you have to do is drop them in the toast-
er and wait till they popped up and your breakfast was
ready."

"You ain't talking about pancakes, man, you're
talking about waffles, ain't you?" Willie asked, as the
men talked, completely ignoring Sonny.

"Yeah man, yeah. You're right! That's what it was, waffles. I don't know where I got that pancake shit at anyway. It must be because I was thinking about them pancakes they serve every Saturday up at the joint. Yeah, man, that's what it was. My mind was on them hip pancakes."

"Your mind is going to be on more than any pancakes, peckerwood, if you don't set out a pack of cigarettes to make up for my cornflakes you're eating," Sonny said angrily. He had made his choice. He knew he couldn't whip all of them, but one of them had to go if he was to retain his respect on the ward.

"Man, I didn't take your cornflakes, Sonny, so I don't owe you a fuckin' thing!" Tony replied sharply. He knew what Sonny was trying to do, and it made him angry that the man had picked him out of the bunch as the weak one. All of his life he had never been ashamed of being white, but for once he wished desperately that his skin was coal black. If someone had told him a year ago that he'd one day wish that he was a black man, he'd have looked at the man as if he was losing his mind.

"Duane Jefferson? Get your clothes together; you're on your way to Jackson," the deputy roared from the front of the rock. The men had been so engrossed in their petty argument that none of them had noticed the door to their rock being unlocked. The deputy came down the corridor, stopping at each ward. Each one had at least one man waiting for the shipment to Jackson.

Preacher quickly rolled up his belongings and

walked over to where Chester was. "Is it really true, brother, that you can't take anything inside the wall with you?"

"Just your bare ass, Preach. When you get there, they'll make you undress in the first building you go in, and they give you a shower. When you take that shit off you got on, you'll never see it again until you get ready to leave." Damn, Chester swore to himself. He had forgot that Preacher had gotten life. The man would never leave the place until the day he died, then they'd take him out the back way and bury him on the little hill behind the prison. "They even take your cigarettes, Preach," Chester added quickly to cover up his blunder. "You get a bath, haircut, and a brand new outfit of white coveralls that you'll be sick of before you even put them on."

All of the men in the ward were listening now. "You don't have to worry about the white outfit, though. You won't have it on but for a day. They take your measurements the same day you get there, and by the next day, some inmate will come around and give you some brand-new blue work clothes. Two outfits, plus a pair of shoes and socks. Oh yeah, man, they really take care of their new arrivals." Chester glanced at the books Preacher held under his arm. "I'm sorry, man, about them books you got there. They won't do nothing but take them from you and throw them away."

Preacher glanced fondly at the books and writing paper he held. Tears appeared in the corners of his eyes. "You mean I can't even take my personal mail in?" he asked, his voice breaking slightly.

It was difficult to watch the man. He was on the verge of breaking. "Nothing," Chester said, turning away from Preacher as he spoke, not wanting to see the hurt in the man's eyes. "The first time I went to Jackson, Preacher, I bought a whole carton of cigarettes so that I would have them in quarantine; man, you know I must have been broken-hearted when them jive-ass motherfuckers took every goddamn pack of them. I figured, like most guys do who never have been there before, that if they weren't open, they'd let you keep them. But it don't go like that. They take everything."

Preacher sighed, "Well, if that's the case...," he said and began unrolling his bag. He took out four packs of cigarettes, two candy bars and a pack of cupcakes and started to pass them around.

Sonny held his hand out. Preacher glanced up at the man and pure hatred jumped out of his eyes. Neither man had spoken to the other since the warning Preacher had given the younger man. Now they glared at each other. The candy bar that Preacher had started to put into the outstretched hand was immediately given to another. Knowing the man had just gotten through arguing with Tony, Preacher made it a point to take the candy bar and give it to Tony.

The sound of the deputy coming back caused the tension in the ward to disappear. Men who had anticipated trouble began to relax. The deputy stopped at their door. "Break two!" he yelled and waited until Preacher had stepped through the door before going on down the rock towards the other wards. "You can wait here if you want to," he said casually, as he walked on down the catwalk.

Preacher stood outside the ward gossiping with the men jammed against the bars. In those short minutes, Preacher did more talking to the other men than he had done during his long confinement in the ward.

When the deputy came back up the catwalk, followed by three other men, he stopped. "You guys due in court this morning get ready. As soon as we get these men shipped out of here, I'll be back for you guys going to court."

Preacher waved once, then followed the other men down the catwalk. The door had hardly closed before Sonny began to resume the argument. "Hey, man, I don't want to be hard to get along with, so I'll tell you what I'll do. You give up the candy bar and I'll forget about the pack of cigarettes I asked you for." Before Tony could reply, he continued, "I believe that's fair, man. Since you didn't even pay for that candy, it shouldn't be no problem. I ain't had nothing to eat this mornin'. You guys split up my food, so fair is fair." He motioned towards the watching men. "Ask any of them guys. See what they say." Sonny knew if any of the watching men were asked, they would take his side, because they feared him, whereas they had no reason to fear Chester's group.

Tony relented. It would be the easy way out, he thought. Give up the candy bar and it was over with. He didn't fear Sonny, but since he was due in court in a few hours, he didn't want any form of trouble.

"Here, man, have fun," he said and tossed the candy bar to Sonny.

His action surprised Chester. That was the last thing Chester had expected to happen. He glanced at his white friend. The unspoken question was in his eyes. Why? Chester knew, or rather he believed, that fear had nothing to do with it. No, he had seen Tony in action, so he didn't believe that Tony was afraid to tangle with Sonny.

"I'm due in court this morning, man," Tony said, answering the question that was in Willie and Chester's minds but hadn't been asked. "It don't make sense having any trouble today, not this day anyway. I didn't tell you guys, but my lawyer says there might be a small chance to get probation—if he can get my charge dropped to attempted armed robbery." Tony couldn't understand the funny expressions that flashed across his friends' faces at his words.

Only another black man could really understand what went through the minds of the two listening men. It wasn't that they would resent his making probation, because they definitely would resent it, but not for any reasons that he would grasp immediately. It would take time and patience to explain it to him, then he still might not understand.

"That's great, man, just great," Willie managed to say. "I just wish I was that lucky. My fuckin' lawyer is talking shit about coppin' out, and maybe, just maybe, he might be able to get me a ten-year max."

"Ain't no sense you foolin' yourself, Willie," Chester began softly. "If your lawyer did tell you some shit about probation, you'd laugh in his face, 'cause you know ain't no way in the hell for the judge to give you probation with your record."

"Hold it a minute, Chester," Tony blubbered, trying to break the tension he felt but couldn't understand. "My record is just as bad as Willie's. We've both done prison bits before, each one of us have been in juvenile, and we're both charged with an armed robbery this time." Tony looked at the men, confident that Willie had a chance too. "There's another thing in Willie's favor, too. Don't forget, there was violence in my case. That foolish-ass Gene shot a guy in the leg, whereas in Willie's armed robbery, there was no violence whatsoever." He glanced at the two men, making sure they were listening to his words. "I mean, it's as plain as day. If Willie can get his case broke down to attempted armed robbery, he'd stand a chance of getting probation, too. I mean, it ain't no cut-and-dried thing. There isn't any guarantee that I'm going to get it, but the point I'm trying to get across to you guys is that the chance is there."

Chester shrugged. "Yeah, baby boy, I dig where you're coming from now," Chester said, not meaning a word of what he said. "At first, I didn't dig it, but now I understand what you mean. Keep the faith, that's all, just keep the faith." He grinned as he coldly thought: It's easy for a white boy to walk over to the courtroom with such an idea in his mind, probation. But for a nigger to do it was sheer stupidity. All he would be doing would be fooling himself, looking for something that wasn't about to happen, unless he was an informer or something.

The sounds of the front doors on the catwalk opening came to the men. They glanced at each other. It seemed a little early to be going over to court, but one never knew. They took the men over early to court, true enough, but their built-in alarm clocks told them it was just too early yet. The breakfast bowls hadn't been picked up yet, even. The men never went over until after the trays were picked up from each ward. This was one of the ways they told time, how they knew it was still too early to be going to court.

Pete, the black deputy that worked the morning shift, came back to their cell. He just stood and stared inside the cellblock without speaking. Suddenly he raised his head and pointed, "I don't know who put their shit on top of Preacher's bunk, but whoever did it, they had better get it off." The men inside the ward stared at him stupidly. They heard him but couldn't understand him. The deputies never interfered in the bunk arrangements inside the wards. They left it up to the men to handle it themselves. But there was one thing they couldn't overlook. Pete had given an order, and that meant it was to be obeyed. Pete was the kind of guard you could talk to, even get him to mail a letter for you, if you knew him well enough, but he was also a guard that never let you forget your place. You were the prisoner; he was the guard. He never joked with the men, or about the men. When he gave an order, he meant it.

William Cather, one of the white inmates, didn't waste any time. He picked his belongings back up off the bunk and moved back to his mattress on the floor. It had been too good to be true anyway, he reasoned. He hadn't expected to be able to hold on to a bunk. Sooner or later one of the new colored boys sleeping on the floor would have taken his bunk, so now he didn't have that problem to worry about. He didn't understand why the deputy had done it, but by the same token, he didn't think the deputy realized what he had really done. William had waited two months for that opening; now, because of the deputy's interference, he'd lose his turn. As far as the rest of the men were concerned, the bunk was his; if he lost it, that was his problem.

Two deputies came up to the cellblock, dragging and half carrying an inmate between them. "This guy just came out of the hospital," Pete informed the prisoners as he unlocked the door, "so he needs a bunk to sleep on." He opened the door and stood back as the guards pushed the man through the opening.

"The bunk over there next to the face bowl is yours, Walker. The one on the bottom," Peter said to the badly battered man. Walker's face was covered with large, red, vivid bruises. It appeared as though someone had beaten the man with a flat object, something that left huge marks. David Walker was a light-complexioned Negro, so the marks showed up more vividly than they would had he been darker.

Walker staggered in the direction of the pointing finger, and someone grabbed his elbow and steered him over to the bunk, where he fell out for dead, unaware of the hum of speculation about him that began as soon as the deputies went back to their other duties. He didn't even awaken when, a short while later, the deputy came through calling out the names of the few men who were due to go across the street to have their brief moments in court.

8

THE EVENING HAD started out like most summer evenings for David and his friends. On the fifth bottle of wine, Ed, the smaller of the two men in the front seat suggested that they stop in at a topless bar.

"Hey, Duke, why don't you drive out on Seven Mile Road? They got a mean bitch out there dancing. I was out there last week and saw the tits on the broad. You can't believe it, man!" He cupped both hands to add emphasis. "Out here, baby! The bitch's tits are bigger than Robert's head."

Both men laughed. The driver, Robert, took the kidding good-naturedly. He reached up and rubbed his head, which was rather odd shaped, shaped like a football, but he was accustomed to remarks about his long head. What he didn't like was the use of his name, Robert. He liked to be called Duke, ever since he had gone to the movie as a young boy and had seen a picture with James Cagney—a gangster picture in which Cagney had been called Duke. Ever since then, whenever he introduced himself, he told people his name was Duke. Only the very oldest of his friends knew that his real name was Robert Williams. Also, only the very oldest and closest friends ever called him anything else but Duke.

"How much wine is left in the bottle?" Duke asked as he drove down a ramp, getting onto the freeway.

"Shit," David said half drunkenly, "with you long throat motherfuckers, how much wine do you think is left in the bottle?" To add emphasis to his words, he raised the bottle and drained the rest of the wine without bringing the bottle down. When he did, it was completely empty.

"You greedy bastard!" Ed said, twisting around in his seat. "You don't think of nobody but your goddamn self!"

"Fuck it, baby, all we got to do is stop and pick up another one. You know David ain't happy unless his goddamn head is down between his knees," Duke stated, not really caring about his friend drinking up the last of the wine. "What we goin' do, take a bottle inside the bar with us and pour our drinks under the table?"

"You goddamn right," David said. "I ain't goin' sit in there and pay no fuckin' dollar a bottle every time we order a beer."

"Why don't we pick up a pint of whiskey?" Ed asked. "It wouldn't be no problem pouring it under the table like the wine would be."

Duke read the freeway signs and turned off at the next ramp. "I just don't want to pay no kind of cover charge, man. If they got one, we goin' have to bypass the big tits and all," Duke said as he expertly drove the car through the evening traffic. He sighted a liquor store and pulled over and parked. "We might as well get the cash together," he said as he removed a dollar bill from his pocket. "Let's get a pint of Johnnie Walker Red. Ain't no sense in drinking cheap whiskey on top of all that wine we done poured down."

The men pretended that it cost too much, signifying back and forth between themselves until they tired of the number and produced the money. Ed, small, thin and dark, grinned as he got out of the car to go into the store, revealing the gap between his teeth. "At least I'll get to keep the change," he said casually, laughing at his partners' faces.

They drove on towards the bar, not bothering to open the bottle of whiskey until after they reached the Top Hat nightclub. The men sat through the first floor show, but they didn't see the girl Ed had bragged about. After asking one of the waitresses about her, they finished their drinks and left.

"Goddamn it," Ed cursed as they left the bar. "How the fuck was I to know the dumb bitch quit her job? With tits like hers, she should stay in a bar displaying them."

"Yeah, man, yeah," David said drunkenly. "Them goddamn tits is what's got us out of our money. Ten dollars blowed across the bar, and for what?" he asked as he turned up the whiskey bottle and drank straight from the bottle.

Duke glared at him. "Take it easy, baby. What you trying to do, find your mammy in the bottom of the bottle?" he asked sharply, stopping for a red light. He glanced over at the man sitting in the front seat with him. "You goin' end up being a fuckin' alcoholic, Dave," he stated seriously.

David brought the bottle down. "Man, I ain't no damn drunk. I just like to feel my shit when I drink, that's all." He took a short swig out of the bottle before anybody could stop him.

"Let the greedy bastard go," Ed said from the back-seat. "If you see a beer store, pull over and I'll pick up some cold beer."

The men rode in silence, each watching the store fronts as they passed, making sure they didn't pass up the beer store. It was still early, not yet midnight. "There's one over on your right, Duke," Ed yelled, pointing out at the store.

David's head came up off his chest, where it had been resting. "What y'all goin' get? Some wine or some more whiskey?" His words were becoming slurred.

Both men ignored him, not even bothering to answer or to ask him for his money. Ed jumped out and ran inside the beer and wine store. Duke twisted the dial on the radio until he found some soul music.

He popped his fingers along with the tune playing. He glanced up once or twice after the tune went off and another had played, wondering what was taking Ed so long.

Suddenly Ed appeared, steering a drunken white woman along. He seemed to be holding her up by her elbows. When he reached the car door, Duke had to reach over and pull David out of the way. David had fallen asleep, leaning against the door. "Move over, man," he yelled as he tugged at the drunken man. He managed to roll him over on the seat as Ed climbed in, still clutching the woman's arm.

Duke stared at the white woman. She looked to be in her late thirties or early forties, he didn't know which. Her hair was a dirty blonde color, dyed. He could see the brown roots showing. Her wide grin revealed dirty teeth, while an odor of stale beer and wine came from her. Her clothes were wrinkled, as if she had slept in them. She had large legs, while still maintaining some sort of shape. Her breasts were huge mountains of white flesh, which bulged under the thin cotton blouse she wore.

"Well I'll be damn," Duke managed to say. "What the hell have we got here, Ed?" he asked curiously.

"I run into her inside the store, Duke. She asked me to buy her a bottle of wine, so I asked her if she wanted to ride with us and drink it." Ed made a gesture towards the bag, where two bottles of wine could be seen. As he spoke, his hands fondled the woman's breasts. Duke pulled away from the curb, and a joyous warmth invaded his private parts as he realized that the night wouldn't be a blank after all.

The woman leaned over and kissed Ed. "How about pouring me a cup of that stuff, honey?" she asked in a harsh whisper. "Poor Jean's throat is sure dry," she added.

Ed opened the wine and poured her out a cupful. She drank it down straight and held her cup out again before he could finish pouring a drink for Duke and himself. He refilled her cup, then asked, "We goin' have a little fun later on, ain't we, Jean?" His voice shook as he waited for her reply.

For an answer, she took his hand and placed it between her legs, then closed her legs. "You can bet on it, honey," she said, then tossed the cup of wine down. "You didn't get any beer, did you?" she asked, rummaging through the bag to see for herself.

It was becoming more difficult for Duke to concentrate on his driving. In his rearview mirror, he watched Ed's hands fondling the woman's body, and his penis became swollen. He forced his eyes from the mirror and gritted his teeth tightly. Have patience, he told himself over and over again.

On the second bottle of wine, David woke up enough to ask for a cup, but before it was poured out, he had fallen asleep again. Nobody bothered to awaken him.

"How about us gettin' some more wine?" Jean asked as they drove into an alley.

"We can get the wine later," Duke said. "Let's take care of this other business first, okay?"

Jean studied Duke closely. All she could see was

a black man with a huge head and red eyes. She decided to get it over with quickly. She had known what the men wanted from the first. There was no squeamishness in her; she rather looked forward to balling the two young black men. Her only regret was that they were out of wine. She stretched out on the backseat, and immediately Ed climbed between her legs. He didn't bother to take his pants down; he just unzipped his fly.

"Harder, you black bastard, fuck me harder!" the woman yelled. Duke glanced over at David; his friend never even opened his eyes. "Oh Jesus, you little-dick sonovabitch!" she screamed.

Duke glanced out of the car windows uneasily. He had parked in an alley behind a vacant house, but she was carrying on so loud that it scared him. The sight of Ed climbing off the woman ended his slight fear. As Ed climbed out of the car, Duke made his way onto the backseat.

"Oh yes, daddy," she said as he unzipped his pants, revealing a large, swollen penis She grabbed it and pulled him down on top of her, not giving him time to pull his pants down. "Now this is more like it," she said as he began to move his hips. "Give it all to me, boy," she screamed; her voice took on a southern accent. "Goddam it, nigger, give it all to me! More. More," she gasped, pulling on his thin hips.

David moaned on the front seat, turned over, and began to snore loudly. The noise coming from the backseat never disturbed him. It was as though he was in another world, which he was—the world of the drunk completely enveloped in his own stupor.

The sudden bright lights of another car pinned Ed to the rear of the car, where he stood trying to clean up his pants. He glanced up in panic. The first thing he noticed was the police sign on the car. Fear gripped him, and he could feel his stomach tighten. His fear of the police overcame his common sense.

As the policemen got out of the car and came towards them, Jean lifted her head and glanced out the back window. As soon as she saw the police, she screamed loudly. The sound of her scream made up Ed's mind for him. He did what he had thought about doing at first: he ran. There was no place for him to go but straight down the alley. The sounds of the policemen's guns never reached him, because he was suddenly hit in the back by a blow that lifted him from his feet and sent him skipping across the asphalt, face down. He never felt the other bullets that struck him, either. The first one had taken his life.

Instinctively, Duke came out of the backseat quickly, but after being a witness to what happened to Ed, he had enough sense not to run. He put both his hands over his head and stood beside the car, trembling with fear.

One of the officers held a gun on them while the other one went down the alley and turned Ed's body over with his foot. When he came back, he remarked, "Well, that's one good nigger down the alley now. He won't be bothering anyone any damn more."

After that, it seemed a nightmare to Duke. Another police car pulled into the alley, and to make matters worse, both of its occupants were white too. Duke cursed quietly as he watched the white men pull David from the car. He was still too drunk to stand up, but it didn't stop them from punching on him. When David fell to the ground, the officers seemed to take pleasure in kicking the helpless man.

The arrival of two black policemen stopped some of the unnecessary brutality. They watched the proceedings for a few minutes, then one of the black officers spoke up. His voice was controlled, but it was threaded with that quality of controlled wrath that only a fool couldn't recognize. "We might as well take these guys down to the hospital, then book them," he said, as he began pushing Duke towards their police car. His partner managed to get David on his feet and guide him to their car.

The two black officers didn't bother with the white woman; they left her in the care of their fellow officers. As the driver of their car started up the motor, his headlights picked up the body of Ed, still lying in the middle of the alley. He eyed the body for a moment, then said with grim resignation: "Well, I guess it's a good thing we came back here when we did, or there'd probably be more than one black man stretched out dead in this alley."

"Yeah," his partner answered sharply, "and all for a piece of white ass!"

That evening, David joined Chester and the others at county jail.

9

SUNDAY MORNING IS the morning of leisure for most people, but for the men incarcerated, it is just another day—or rather, an extra slow day. The only thing the men had to look forward to was visiting time. Since early morning, the men had started getting ready for their visits, combing and recombing their hair and pressing faded prison blue jeans—coaxing slight creases into the thin, worn fabric.

With an amused grin, Chester watched the men getting ready. It always surprised him to see the trouble the men went through, when it was obvious that the visitors that came to see them couldn't see what they wore. It wouldn't have made any difference if they sat in the visiting room stark naked; the people stand-ing outside couldn't see anything but their faces. They had to talk to each other by phone.

It must be, he thought, that it didn't make any dif-ference if the visitors could see them or not. The only thing the inmates were interested in was killing time. And that's exactly what pressing the old blue jeans did for them—gave them something to do. Some of the men had other clothes. They had their suits that they kept clean, so that whenever they did go to court, their appearance wouldn't be too trampish—as if that made any difference.

There was another farcical endeavor the men went through, going to the trouble of having their people go out and buy them brand new suits to wear to court. Courts never took into consideration what the men had on. They could appear in sacks, for all the judges cared. The only thing that mattered was the color of the man, plus what he was charged with. The men going to court never bothered to think that the money their mothers and wives had to spend on them could be used for something else. Put food on tables that had seen more than their share of black-eyed peas and navy beans—wihout meat. Yet these same women had to figure out a way to buy their loved ones a suit, a good suit at that.

None of the men would think of wearing a cheap suit. No, and the women knew this. They had to try and buy the best. They had to spend at least a hun-dred dollars or better, because they knew their men would look at the label before even putting it on. But the comical aspect was the misguided belief of the women that this would help their men. Some of them had to take their whole welfare checks to buy the suits. They sacrificed everything under the misguided belief that it would help. How could it? What could help against the poisonous pus of double-standard justice, racial bigotry, and the demand for black men to fill the work quotas? Many men were needed at a certain time of the year to help pick the fields—corn fields, potatoes and what have you. These things couldn't be left to rot; they had to be picked.

Damn it all, Chester swore under his breath as he stretched out on his bunk. How stupid can our people be? Can't they see this shit? It's as plain as day, but yet they continue to fool themselves.

"Hey, baby, what you goin' do, man, sleep the whole damn day away?" Willie asked as he stood at the foot of Chester's bed, grinning down at the man.

"What is it, blood? I see you done went and got sharp. You must be expecting a visit today," Chester replied as he opened his eyes, wishing Willie would disappear. He was in one of his moods where he didn't want to be disturbed by anyone.

"Come on, Chester, roll out of that fuckin' bunk," Tony said. "I been waitin' all morning so we could get our chess game on with." He held out a lit cigarette to Chester as the man pretended to slowly awaken.

With difficulty, Chester managed to take the smoke. He slowly inhaled, then blew the smoke out. "What's the matter with you guys? Don't you ever sleep? We just finished a wonderful meal," he said, referring to the noon meal that they had just eaten. On Sundays their noon meal was the best one of the week, either ham, roast beef, or chicken, with mashed potatoes or corn. No other meal through the week compared with Sunday's.

"I saved a ham sandwich, Chester," Willie said. "You want part of it?" Before Chester could reply, Willie produced the sandwich.

Tony walked over to his bed, reached under his pillow, and came back towards the man, shaking an illegal plastic jug. The contents of the jug splashed around as he shook it. The other men in the ward watched him closely.

"What the hell have you got there?" Chester asked curiously. His surprise was total; he even sat up in his bunk. He tried to control his delight, because if it was what he thought it was, it would really be a treat.

"We got us a whole quart of spud juice," Tony said, then added quietly so that no one could overhear, "I bought it from one of the trusties. You know the blond kid that sweeps the catwalks? He pressed it on me for a box of smokes."

Chester grinned. "Spud juice! Well, now, this might just turn into a damn good day after all. But you done blowed all your smokes, ain't you?"

Tony returned his grin. "Yeah, man, I kind of hurt my stash, but seeing as how I go to court tomorrow for sentence, I won't be needin' that many anyway. Either way, if I get some time, I'll be riding out to Jackson sometime this week—or I'll be out on probation, if my lawyer ain't shittin' me."

Willie caught Chester's eye as he began to speak. "This cat still believes we might get probation, Chester. That's all he talks about when we go across the street. In fact, he's talked me into taking a cop, pleading guilty to attempted armed robbery."

"What!?" Chester roared loudly, then caught himself. "Man, are you losing your fuckin' mind?" Chester glared at Willie as if he were insane. "Don't you know, Willie, that you can get life in prison for that charge? Yeah, I'm hip it carries a floatin' max, plus that shit about probation, but man, it still carries a life sentence if the judge wants to give it to you."

Willie looked around sheepishly. "I know all that, Chester, but they was goin' find me guilty anyway, so I took my chances this way. I talked to the probation man, too," he added, as if this would make a big difference.

Tony, conscious of the fiery look that was in Chester's eyes, hesitated, then held out the jug of spud juice. "How about you guys taking a drink with me?"

For a brief moment, Chester started to crush the jug, then thought better of it. It wasn't Tony's fault—nor Willie's, for that matter. Both men wanted to get out, and each thought he was doing the right thing. But from experience, Chester believed that Willie had fucked himself up. For Tony, a guilty plea wouldn't go too bad. He had a chance. With his record, Chester didn't believe he'd get out on paper, but he didn't believe he'd get the same time that Willie got, even though both men had the same charge. In fact, he

looked forward to seeing the outcome of it and wondered how each man would come out.

"I'll make you a bet, Tony," Chester said as he took
a long drink out of the jug. "Damn! This some good
spud juice. Whoever made it knew their business.
Anyway, I'll bet you a box of smokes, Tony, that even
though your record is worse than Willie's, you'll get
less time than he does."

Tony rubbed his jaw as he thought the matter over,
then grinned. "I think I'll just take that box from you,
Chester. You're forgettin' that there was violence in
my case. Willie didn't even shoot his gun into the
floor. That makes a lot of difference, Chester, a hell
of a lot of difference."

"Well then, I guess you don't mind taking that box
bet after all. If you think Willie has that good a chance,
you might as well clean up along the way," Chester
said.

For a second, Tony was uneasy. He didn't know
why, but he realized that Chester was mad about
something. He decided to make the bet just to keep
Chester happy. If he won, he wouldn't even accept
the carton of cigarettes. "Okay, man," he said finally.
"You got a bet. Willie ain't about to get as much time
as I'm going to get tomorrow."

The men passed the jug back and forth until it was
just about empty. Willie broke out his ham sandwich
and all of them took a small piece. "Shit, this is better than downtown," Willie stated loudly as he
observed the other inmates watching them enviously.

An old, white alcoholic made his way over to where

they were partying. He spoke directly to Tony. "Hey, kid, why don't you give an old vet a little swig of that juice, huh? You know how it is when a guy gets in this joint. It's a real pleasure when somebody on the rock gets ahold of something and shares it with his buddies. I mean, you know, I'll return the favor for you one of these days. I'm working on something now. I might just get some real stuff in here. Yes sir, I mean some real stuff." He smacked his lips as his eyes went to the jug, trying to measure how much was left. His eyes watered as he stared at the jug, then his hands began to shake.

"There ain't enough here, mac," Tony answered sharply as he held the jug out to Willie.

The old bum almost cried as he watched Willie turn the jug up. He turned on Tony in a rage, his anger getting the best of his judgment. He had been around too long to make the kind of mistake he made. "By God!" he roared, "You'd give a drink to a coon before…." He caught himself. At once he realized his mistake. From the look that flashed across Willie's face, he knew he had made a *terrible* mistake. He tried to grin. "Boy," he began, as Willie stood up, "I didn't mean no harm. That's just a term we use where I come from."

Willie's hand moved like a blur. Once, twice, he slapped the old white man viciously across the face. "You sonofabitch! As long as I'm in this ward, honkie, you better stay the fuck out of my way!" Grabbing the man's shirt tightly, Willie gave him a shove, and the man stumbled and fell. He didn't bother to look back as he scrambled to his feet. He just got up and ran back to the corner he stayed in with the rest of the wineheads.

Chester killed the rest of the spud juice. "Well, now, I guess we can relax and enjoy our high now." The small group of men laughed, breaking the tension that had been building.

*   *   *

Later that evening, Willie got up and left to take his shower so that he would be ready for court in the morning. Tony sat on the edge of Chester's bed for a few more minutes, but as the conversation began to drag, he made his excuse and went off to take his shower too.

Chester stretched out on his narrow bunk. He was glad that the men had finally left him. At times too much company gave him a headache. As soon as he closed his eyes, he slipped off into an unwholesome slumber. Instantly his clothes were soaked with perspiration as he relived in his dream the fateful day of his wife's misfortune. Almost imperceptibly he began to grit his teeth in his sleep. The noise drew attention to his sleeping form, but he was unaware of it.

*   *   *

He could see the matronly shaped, heavyset woman sitting in the front of the boat. Slowly, then more openly as he found it difficult to tilt the boat, he rocked back and forth. As she opened her mouth to ask what he was doing, he managed to tilt the boat, and as he went overboard, he grabbed the side to make sure it tilted all the way. She came out of the boat with a loud splash, then started to scream. Chester pictured himself diving, swimming underwater until he saw her feet, then grabbing one of them as he attempted to drag her under. He remembered, as he broke out into a cold sweat, the feeling of her shoe as she kicked at him frantically in her attempt to break his grip on her foot. Slowly his lungs began to feel as if they would burst from lack of air. He forced himself to stay under, clutching her foot, until he couldn't stand it any longer. He released her and swam up.

When his head cleared the surface of the water, he sucked in air in deep gasps. Suddenly her head came up a few feet from his, and sudden fear filled his heart as he thought of the crime he was committing and what she would say if they got ashore.

Quickly his eyes searched the nearby shore. He could see a few people standing at the edge of the water. As an overwhelming conviction that he had blown it filled him, he noticed out of the corner of his eye that his wife had gone under again. She's too damn fat to drown, he thought. She'll only float. As the thought flashed across his mind, he could hear someone calling out for them to hold on. He decided against going back under and attempting to hold her under. It was too risky. He grabbed ahold of the overturned boat and held on.

As he clutched at the boat, he watched a canoe put out from the shore. The two men inside the small boat were paddling frantically to reach him. Chester cursed under his breath and glanced around momentarily to see where his wife was. She was nowhere in sight. A feeling of sweet exhilaration overcame him as he opened his mouth and began to yell for help. The closer the boat approached, the louder he yelled. As an arm finally grabbed him, he started to struggle and yell over and over again, "Get my wife first! Help her!" The strength of the grip on his arm increased as he yelled, "Help my wife! Help my wife!"

He opened his eyes and stared up at the naked Willie, who stood over him, shaking him roughly.

* * *

"Wake up, baby, you're screaming your head off," Willie said as the enveloping sleep disappeared from Chester's eyes and the man came fully awake. "Them must be some hell of a dreams you have, brother," Willie said lightly.

Chester sat up quickly, then lit a cigarette. As he slowly took a drag off the smoke, parts of his dream came back to him. The only difference between his dream and a nightmare was that his dream really happened. He tried to blank the pictures out of his mind, but he remembered too clearly the two men in the boat and the time they spent trying to locate his wife's body. After a while he had jumped back in the water to make it look good. He went underwater searching for the body. He came up once and the men tried to get him to come back into the boat, but he had dived again. This time he came upon her body, caught at the bottom in some weeds. He pried her loose and dragged the heavy body towards the boat. He remembered thinking how difficult it was to tow her along. He had always thought that fat people floated, or that a body would float to the top if left alone, but he found it hard to drag her to the top again. Her weight, or the muddy water he was swimming in, made the going difficult. He found himself fighting for air and he started to turn the body loose and swim up by himself, but before he could make up his mind, his head finally cleared the surface. The two men paddled over and helped him with the heavy woman. The three of them had a time trying to get the fat woman's body inside the small canoe. At one time they almost capsized, but finally they managed to get her aboard.

Chester shook the thoughts from his head. "Yeah, baby boy," he said to Willie, "it's one hell of a nightmare I have. Maybe one day I'll run it down to you."

"That's all right, my man, I have enough nightmares of my own without hearing about yours," Willie said with a smile. "I'm afraid if you tell it to me, I might fuck around and have the same one myself."

Both men laughed as Willie grinned down on Chester. "I guess you'll be all right now," he said as he walked over to his bunk and picked up his towel and finished drying himself off.

"Goddamn," Chester stated, grinning, "no wonder I had a nightmare. I must have seen you walk past my bunk with all that meat swinging and it put the fear of God in me. Boy, you cover up when you come out of that damn shower. Shit, I won't be the only one in here having nightmares if you keep walking around with all that dick hanging. Shit, you'll be done scared the shit out of one of these kids that done heard that they'd get raped if they ever got in the county jail."

Willie grinned back at Chester as he stretched out on his bunk. He was proud of the way he was hung, and it made him happy that Chester had referred to how large he was hung in front of the other men. He settled down on his bunk, and in a matter of a few minutes he was snoring softly.

For a while, Chester lay awake thinking of his recurring nightmare. As he smoked cigarette after cigarette, he silently watched the men who were too ashamed to use the community toilet in the daytime. Each in turn got up from their bunks and slipped over to the toilet. He smiled to himself in the semi-darkness. It never really got dark in the ward, but they did turn off a few of the lights.

Chester was still awake when the changing of the guards took place. He listened as the new guard made his rounds. His footsteps could be heard as he made his way down the back of the catwalks. Chester heard him three minutes before the guard passed their ward, flashing his flashlight inside to see if he could see anything. No wonder the bastards can't ever catch nobody fuckin', he thought to himself for what seemed like the thousandth time since he had been locked up.

As he lit another cigarette, he glanced around at the sleeping figures. Some of the men were sleeping on ditty mattresses, while others had filthy blankets drawn up over them to keep out the early-morning chill. Roaches ran about the floor in what seemed like packs, after the food crumbs the men tossed about with utter disregard. As Chester watched, one sleeping man awoke with a curse, beating at his blankets. A small mouse ran from under his cover and out through the open bars. The man continued to curse loudly until another sleeping figure yelled for him to shut up.

Well, it's Monday, anyway, Chester observed to himself drily as he rolled up in his blanket and tried to regain the temporary relief of sleep.

10

THE MEN BEGAN THE new day by sweeping. They didn't have a broom, so they used magazines and a piece of cardboard to sweep the cigarette butts and other debris into a pile. One of the old bums went through the pile of rubbish slowly, searching for discarded cigarette butts.

"Goddamn it!" another inmate cursed, "how fuckin' long you goin' stay on that shitter? Somebody else might want to shit this morning, too!"

The man using the toilet ignored the outburst. He continued to take his time, reading an old newspaper spread across his lap. He sat there as if he were at home. He farted loudly and looked up grinning. The

few men still eating their breakfast scowled and
looked away.

"Why don't you put some water with that shit?"
Willie yelled from his bunk. He turned his back on
the man, but in a moment the sound of the toilet being
flushed could be heard.

"You might think I'm playing, but I'm dead serious, my man. I got to use that toilet, so you better get
your head out of that fuckin' paper and get up off that
shitter," the man who had spoken earlier said. He
stood over the man on the toilet, his fists clenched.

Chester lit his morning cigarette and watched the
two black men. It could turn into something nasty if
one of them didn't give in. The man on the toilet
decided that he wasn't in the best of positions for a
fight, so he began to make preparations to get up.
"Okay, baby, I'm just about finished," he said as he
searched for some toilet paper.

"Here, brother," the other man said as he held out
some toilet paper. Each man tried to keep his own roll
of toilet paper, or he'd end up not having any. As soon
as the rolls were put in, the men grabbed them up.

The sound of the turnkey opening the door started
the men to yelling. "Hey, turnkey, how about putting
the mop bucket in here? We ain't been able to clean
up in a week."

"Okay, okay," the guard said as he came back down
the catwalk. "I'll try and get the mop and bucket to
you guys a little later. Just hold on." He continued on
down the rock. At the last ward, he started to call out
names. When he got back up to Chester's ward, he

called out the names of the men due in court that morning.

Willie grinned and got up off his bunk. "Well, Chester, today's the big day. At least it will all be over for me anyway," he said lightly. He was happy. It was a pleasure to finally go to court for sentence, at least one knew that his stay in the county jail was about over. It made a difference that some of them would be going to prison, but they preferred prison to the filthiness of the county jail.

Tony, dressed and ready, sat down on Chester's bunk. He held out his candy bars. The men sat around eating candy bars and kicking the bullshit back and forth until it was time for them to go to court.

David walked over and sat down on the edge of Chester's bunk. "I wish it was me going to court," he said.

"I don't know why," Willie said as he combed his hair again. "They goin' give you so much time for raping that poor li'l old white gal, that you ain't goin' be able to handle it." He grinned at the fear that flashed across David's face. "Yes, sir," he continued, "you boys just busted that white gal's li'l pussy wide open, so it's goin' go awful bad on you over there."

For a brief moment, Chester felt sorry for David. He had heard the boy's story, even though he didn't really believe it. It was hard to believe that he hadn't done anything but was still charged with rape. The sight of the man's beaten face was enough to bring pity out of a person. This was the first time, though, that he had ever felt sorry for a man in jail for rape.

David stuck to his story, and he told it so pitifully, he almost made the hard-hearted men inside the ward believe him. What really gave truth to the story was the fact that the man really claimed he didn't know what had happened that night—except what the police had told him. But what he did know was that he had been dead drunk. This he stuck to. If he had had relations with a woman, he would have known it. But he had been far too drunk.

The sound of the guard coming back caused the men to start milling around the door. "Well," Tony began, "you better order that carton of smokes for me, Chester, 'cause I'll be back to smoke them shortly." He grinned and started towards the door as the turnkey unlocked it.

Willie got up and followed him. "In a minute, baby," he said as he straightened his shoulders and began to cat towards the door. He stopped when he reached the open door and gave the clenched-fist salute, grinned, and catted on down the catwalk.

Chester waited patiently for David to go back to his own bunk, then he stretched out and closed his eyes. He had gotten little sleep, only catnaps, so he closed his eyes. In a minute he was snoring. He was a boy again, walking through the cotton fields of Georgia. He carried the small pack in his arms, clutching it tightly. A farmer's wife had given him the food when he had passed through, after he had cut some wood for her. Now he was making his way down the railroad tracks, eating a piece of the homemade bread she had given him.

The sound of the train coming put fear in his young heart, but he had made up his mind to jump a train so that he could get out of the South. As the train lumbered by, he tossed his package in through an open door, then managed to jump up and pull himself into the boxcar. He had been lucky. The way he had boarded the boxcar showed his inexperience, but some men were not that lucky. For the mistake he had made, he could have fallen beneath the wheels. Suddenly he noticed that the car was not empty. An old, black hobo had already made himself at home. As Chester straightened up, he noticed that the man had his package in his hands and was opening it.

"Go ahead, my man, make yourself welcome," Chester said lightly. He didn't really want to share the food, but since the man had already taken it, he decided to make the best of it.

The hobo grinned and took the last sandwich out of the pack and began to eat it. He didn't bother to offer any to Chester, so Chester turned his back and ignored the man. At first, he wanted to jump back off, but his fear of the southern sheriffs was greater than the fear he held for the old hobo. He felt his pocket, making sure he still had his switchblade.

After a while, the bumping and rocking of the boxcar made him sleepy. He curled up in a corner of the boxcar and quickly fell asleep. Some time later in the evening he felt something touching him in a manner that wasn't right. He jumped awake, only to find himself firmly held from the rear by the strong arms of the hobo.

"Don't carry on so, boy, I ain't goin' hurt you," the hobo said. The man fumbled with the front of his pants, trying to get his pants down around his knees. The strong odor coming from the man's breath filled Chester's nostrils, and he began to struggle silently.

Suddenly the hobo clubbed him on the back of the head with his fist. The blow only added strength to Chester's struggle. Chester had been raised on a farm, so his muscles were firm from the hard work. At times, he had pulled a plow, whenever the mule was too sick to work—which was often, because the mule was very old. So whenever that happened, Chester was put in the mule's harness, along with one of the other young boys who ran around the white man's property.

As the hobo tried to hold him with one hand, Chester grabbed the man's fingers and bent one of them back until he heard a pop. The man let out a scream and rolled away, but it was too late now. Chester was fully angered. He came up on one knee like a cat. The first thing he noticed was the hobo's pants open and his penis hanging out. The sight, and the knowledge of what the man had attempted to do to him, filled him with a blinding rage. He snatched the switchblade from his pocket and flicked it open. The hobo started to beg, but it was too late. The young man moved with the speed of light. His hands were a blur as he thrust the blade into the hobo. The hobo grunted, and Chester struck again. The knife was as bloody as a butcher's working knife as the man slumped to the floor of the boxcar.

Chester leaned against the wall. Not from loss of breath, for he was not even winded. It had been a light workout for him. He could remember many times when he had tussled with his cousin and ended up more tired physically than he was now. It was the finality of his act that completely drained him now. He was too aware of what he had done. No matter that he had acted in self-defense. One of the county sheriffs would throw him in a lockup and it would be anybody's guess when he would ever get off the county chain gang.

He staggered over to the open door and stared out. It was just beginning to get dusk dark. He leaned against the doorjamb until it was so dark out that it was hard to see one's hand in front of one's face. He dragged the body over to the door, but before he pushed it out, he slowly went through the dead man's pockets. It didn't disturb him about robbing the dead. He didn't have any scruples about taking whatever he found. It would help the living, and well did he know that if he didn't take it, the first farmer that came along would relieve the body of whatever it held. He found some loose bills but didn't bother to count them just then. They were passing a deeply wooded section of the land when he pushed the body out of the boxcar.

Chester tried to clean himself up as best he could in the dark, using his handkerchief to wipe the blood from himself and the knife. After that, he stretched out on the hard floor, but sleep eluded him until the steady rumbling of the train induced him to catnap. Money, money, money. That's all he could dream about. As he reached out for it, it seemed to float away from him. He pictured himself in a whiskey store, pistol in hand, telling the white man behind the counter to back up and lean against the wall.

He wasn't a boy this time. His face had a hard cast to it and hawk eyes that seemed to glow. The man hesitated, but when he cocked the hammer on the pistol, the man slowly backed up. He jumped over the counter, gun still in hand, and hit the button that made the cash drawer jump open. Fear leaped into the drug clerk's eyes as Chester ignored the money in the slots and pulled up the container, removing the money from under it. This was the money that the clerk used to cash checks with.

The opening of the outer door to the drug store, the young couple coming in, the fear that leaped into their eyes as they realized that they had walked in on a robbery. Then the boldness of the young man. Chester searched his dream, wondering whether the young white man was trying to impress his girlfriend or if he was just some fool kind of hero. But whichever it was, the man blew the stick-up.

The sudden scream of indignation, the righteous anger that registered on the young man's face as he yelled and charged, then the indefensible mistake on Chester's part—the slight hesitation on his part—that gave the clerk courage. Then the sharp bark of the .38 automatic that he held so tightly gripped in his hand.

It had happened so suddennly. It was over so quickly. The blood flowed down the front of the kid's shirt; the terror in the girlfriend's face as she ran to him, the horror that flashed across the clerk's face as he thought that it was his turn to be shot. Chester had only a moment after that to snatch up as much money as he could, then he broke out and ran. His car was parked around the side, on a small side street, so as soon as he hit the street, he stopped his running and began to walk fast, cursing himself every step of the way because he hadn't taken time to clean out the cash register.

II

THE SOUND OF THE trusties bringing the coffee wagon down the rock brought Chester awake instantly. He sat up and rubbed his eyes. Damn, he reflected, I've been lucky today. I've managed to sleep the whole fuckin' morning away. The arrival of the coffee wagon was a signal to the men that it was time for the afternoon meal. After coffee was passed out, the food came right behind it. Men scurried around the ward in search of containers to hold the hot, steaming liquid. Some of them used empty milk cartons left from breakfast. Others had tin cups, which they guarded as though they were sixteenth-century china. A tin coffee cup with tape around the handle was an extra luxury, something all the men who drank coffee cherished, because it kept the coffee hot. The milk containers though had a tendency to burst at any given minute. Also, they were too hot to handle while the coffee was hot.

Chester took his cup from under the bunk and rinsed it out at the face bowl. He got in line and filled the cup from the large, ten-gallon pot that had been put on their ward. There was always enough coffee to go around but never enough time. The trusties would soon be back, escorted by guards, to pick up the remaining coffee. That was the reason the men tried to get enough containers to have two or three cups of coffee. By the time the chow wagon reached their ward, their coffee would just about be cold. Though they had ways of heating it, they'd have to wait until the guards were passing out food on another rock, because the smell of something burning brought the guards running back like dogs in heat.

Chester took a candy bar from his bunk. He'd been out of sugar for the past two days—since the wagon hadn't been on their ward—so he used candy bars to sweeten the bitter tasting black coffee. First, he had to melt the candy down, then dip it into the coffee until it melted enough so that it wouldn't be lumpy. Chester ate by himself. He didn't want to be bothered. He'd had enough of the banal conversations that the men kept going.

Later in the day, they started bringing back the men from court. Willie and Tony weren't with the first bunch. Two new men were brought to the ward.

Chester lay back listening to the men explain why they were in jail. One of them swore that he'd be out on bond before the day was over. It was the second time that week that he had been arrested. It seemed, from his conversation, that they just came by his house and arrested him for nothing. After searching his home for dope and not finding any, they'd decided to bring him downtown anyway. He swore that he'd been booked three times that month, yet they'd never found any drugs at his home because his wife always flushed the stuff down the toilet before they could kick the front door down. From his conversation, it seemed he didn't open the door fast enough to suit the police, so they always ended up by kicking his door down.

"Hey, blood," Chester called out, getting into the conversation. "Seems as if you could get your lawyer to make them leave you alone, baby boy. The kind of money you have to spend getting out of jail every week should be enough to buy somebody off."

The tall young man stared at Chester coldly. He saw the skeptical way Chester looked at him.

"Hey, my man," he began. "My name is Raymond Wilson, brother, and I don't make it a habit of coming to jail and trying to impress some of these scurrilous half-senile bums you run into on these floors. Like I said, I'll be bailing out tonight, no matter what it costs. Yeah, baby, I'm a dope man too, but one thing you can believe when I tell it to you, when they kicked my door down, they didn't find a goddamn thing!" Raymond hesitated for a minute, then continued. "I wasn't trying to impress, my man, I was just stating a fact. If you'd put up as many bonds this month for nothing as I have, you'd have a fucking attitude too."

The man's anger, his diction, his dress, all of these things Chester became aware of at once. He had made a bad mistake, allowing his anger at his own problems to get in the way of his common sense. He should have noticed at once that this was no ordinary prisoner. Most of the time you could tell by sight the run-of-the-mill prisoner from the rare, exceptional one that came in.

"I'm sorry, Raymond," Chester apologized. "If you stay in here long enough, you'll hear so many bullshit stories that it's hard to see the real from the crap. You know what I mean?"

The tall, slim, brown-skinned man smiled slowly, revealing a mouth full of well-kept, evenly spaced white teeth. He walked over to Chester and pointed to a spot on his bunk. "You mind if I sit with you for a minute, brother?" he inquired in a smooth, velvet voice.

"Knock yourself out, Raymond," Chester replied as he returned the man's smile. "My name is Chester Hines. Most of my friends in here call me Chester." He waited for a second, then added, "Now that we've got that shit out of the way, how about running it down to me. I know how it is at times. I like to get it off my chest at times, too."

The men stared at each other. A mutual understanding instantly flashed between them. "I don't generally take to strangers, Chester, but something about you makes me dig you, man, and I ain't funny."

"I know what you mean, Ray. I think I kind of feel the same thing. It's as if we've known each other for quite a while."

They grinned in unison, then Raymond began speaking slowly. "Some motherfuckin' punk's been talking to the cops about me. They picked some punk up, probably on a thirty-day charge, then the sissy flipped over and gave them my address. I don't sell no drugs from my home, Chester. You know what I mean? My family lives there, man, so I keep it clean. But it don't make no difference. Them honkies come through my home as if I'm dirt! They wouldn't dare treat my white neighbors like that, but since I'm black, it doesn't make no goddamn difference. They don't even have a search warrant. Like tonight, for instance. They come charging through my front door—don't even bother to show their fuckin' badges—give my wife a goddamn cock-and-bull story about somebody called complaining about a disturbance at my house. A fuckin' *disturbance* mind you, but ain't nobody at my house but me and my three kids and wife."

Raymond stopped for a moment, lit a cigarette, then continued. "How about that, nobody but me and my family listening to the LPs. My old lady had just bought a new one by Miles Davis, and we was taking it off. We smoked the last joint in the pad right before they came in. I had a little bit of jam, but I gave the coke to my wife to snort, since it wasn't enough for me to really get turned on with, and she had snorted it before they came in."

For a second there was silence, then Chester asked,

"But what did they book you on, Ray? You know, a meatball, they'd have brought you down and held you for seventy-two hours, then cut you loose. But since you made the county jail, they must have found something to charge you with."

"They did, man, they did!" Ray replied, then laughed coldly, but there was no humor in it. "This is what's so goddamn bitter, baby, dig this. After tearing up the fuckin' house—and I mean *tearing* it up—fucking up the furniture, one jealous-hearted white bastard tossed his lit cigarette on top of the couch, and when my wife rushed over to put it out, the sonofabitch pushed her down!" His voice became harsh as he related the incident. "The bastard pushed her so hard she fell right on her ass. Then all of them motherfuckers tried to look under her skirt since she had on a short mini." Again he hesitated; Chester could tell that he was fighting, trying not to become too emotional as he related what had gone down at his home.

"Yeah, man, when she fell, all them bastards were all eyes. I got a fine black bitch, stacked the way they wished their pale-faced whores were. Anyway, man, after that, I jumped up like a fool, trying to interfere just as they wanted, and the motherfuckers got a chance to knock me on my ass."

He pointed to a bump on his forehead, then continued, "Anyway, they finished searching the house. Now the only goddamn thing they could find was a hypodermic needle that my mother-in-law leaves there. She's got sugar, so she leaves this outfit of hers so that whenever she comes to visit, if she should decide to stay for the night, she has her outfit so that she can take her medicine in the morning. It's that simple. The bastards charged me with possessing a fucking outfit! I guess they'll try and make it look like an outfit that a junkie would use, but neither me or my wife use, so I don't see how they can make a case out of it. We ain't got no tracks, so as soon as I get out, I'll go and see a doctor and have his statement going for me."

Ray shrugged his shoulders, then added, "The cops know they ain't got no case. But it's like the mother-fucker told me, he said I didn't have no business living out there next door to them good white folks, so he's making it his concern that I move my black ass away from out there, if I know what's good for me."

In the silence that followed, Chester thought about what the man had said. He could see where Ray had a problem. If he had been white, they wouldn't have dared treat him like that, but since Raymond was black —living in a damn-near all white neighborhood—they could, and would, do it and get away with it.

"Well, Raymond," Chester said, "what are you planning on doing about it?"

"The only thing I can think of at the moment is to sell out. These fuckin' bonds I'm putting up are beginning to get tiresome. I mean, it adds up after awhile, Chester, but it's not really the money that's bothering me. I can stand a hundred more of these small cases and it wouldn't hurt my bankroll. No, that's not the problem. What I'm worried about is how vulnerable

I am. Them peckerwoods came in my house tonight, pushed my wife around, kicked me in the ass, and one of them slapped my little boy—I guess he was hoping I'd start fighting again; that way he'd have reason to kill me. No, I got the message tonight.

"This is a Little Germany for a black man. Many blacks might not know it, but I do. Hitler couldn't have been much more worse than these white detectives. Here I am afraid to live in a fifty thousand dollar home that I've just about paid for. I'm really, honest to God, afraid to live there. Not just for my black ass but for my family. I mean, if they were to cold-bloodedly kill me, they might just as well kill my wife too. She's black, she's just another black animal to them. The only difference is that they'd love to fuck her, whereas with me they'd just love to shoot the shit out of me. I guess I know now how the Jewish people used to feel in Germany." There was a deep sadness in his voice when he spoke. "You know, Chester, I worked my ass off to get where I'm at. This was my dream come true. A beautiful home, without rats or roaches all over the place. I grew up in the ghetto, man. I saw my baby sister, who was too young to know, eating roaches off the floor. She didn't know any difference, a seven-month-old baby, hungry, waiting on one of the older kids to come back from the store with the milk that my mother had finally gotten the money from another neighbor to buy. Fifty cents, mind you. Fifty fuckin' cents! I've seen the days in my childhood when my mother didn't have fifty cents. So the baby had to go hungry until somebody raised enough money to buy milk. But in the meantime, if she ran into a dead roach on the floor as she crawled around, it was just an ate roach."

As Raymond related this, Chester stared at the floor. What he was saying was what Chester's family was going through now. He hadn't managed to elevate himself from the ghetto yet. It was coming, he believed, but he hadn't managed to do it yet. "I know what you mean, Raymond. I know just what you mean. Shit, I've been in this motherfucker for damn near half a year because I can't raise five hundred dollars."

Raymond glanced away. He caught himself before he made the offer that came to his mind instantly. It would be sheer stupidity to offer to put up that much money for a man that he had just met.

To break the silence that fell between them, Chester asked quietly, "Are you really planning on giving up that beautiful home, Ray?"

Without hesitating, Raymond said, "I'm not ever going to that house again. I wouldn't take the chance of them coming in on me while I was there moving and planting some dope in my pocket. Since they haven't done it yet, I'm not about to allow them the chance to do it now. No, I got the message now. They can have the house. I'll sell it for half of what I paid for it, just to get rid of it. I've learned my damn lesson, brother. When I saw that honkie slap my kid, and I couldn't do nothing about it, I damn near died. It hurt so much, Chester, that I cried, I mean I really cried."

"Shit, if one of them white cocksuckers slapped my kid, I'd kill the motherfucker," a heavyset black man sitting near them stated.

Chester stared at the man. He was new to the ward. He had come in when Raymond did. "I'll just bet you would, Jug," Raymond said, using the man's name. Apparently, Chester thought, they knew each other— or had met down in the bull pen.

That was all it took for the man called Jug to invite himself over. He walked over to the bunk and sat down without asking permission.

Chester glanced at the dirty pants the man wore. "Say, my man, I don't think we know each other, but I don't like a lot of people to sit on my bed. I have to sleep on it, so I make it a point not to have open house."

The man glanced around. "I don't see a lot of people," he said coolly, continuing to sit.

"Well I'll be a motherfucker," Chester said as he rolled over and sat up. "Maybe you didn't understand me, mister, so I'll try again. I sleep here, and I'm used to people asking me before they sit on my bunk."

The man called Jug stared at Chester coldly. He ran his eyes over Chester, examining him closely. He outweighed Chester by at least fifty pounds. "When I come to jail, man, I don't go around asking people's permission about nothing that belongs to the state. Come to think about it, brother, this bunk belongs to the state, so instead of me just sitting on it I might just be sleeping in it before the night's over."

His words brought a silence to the ward. All of the

inmates were watching now. They tried not to do it openly, but they were all watching. Chester examined the fat, black man in front of him. The man was heavy, true enough, but you could tell that he had just started to run to fat. He had tight kinky knots on the top of his head for hair, while his eyes looked like something he had borrowed from a pig. His lips were huge, bluish in color, and the few teeth he possessed were an off-color yellow. There was a long scar around his neck, proof that someone had tried to send him where he belonged.

"Lay off, Jug," Raymond said quietly. "This is a friend of mine. If you must lean on somebody, do it to someone else other than my friend."

Chester hesitated, starting to tell Raymond to stay out of his shit, but he didn't really want any trouble with the man, especially since he was due to go to court that week. He decided to see if Raymond's words carried any weight with the man.

Jug stared at Chester coldly as he got up off the bed. "Okay, Ray baby. If I didn't dig you man, I'd straighten this punk out." Before Chester could reply, the man lumbered off, walking with a so-called hippy swing. Jug was a bully. He didn't mind fighting either. But he had wanted to impress Raymond more than anything else. He had heard about Raymond in the streets. He knew the young man handled a lot of money, and since he wasn't going to be in jail but a few months, he'd planned on trying to tighten their newly acquired friendship up. If he was lucky, Raymond might give him an address where he could

be reached. He believed Raymond needed a man like
him. In his quick daydream, he pictured himself getting tight with Raymond, then sticking him up for
some of that big money it was said Raymond had. But
being honest with himself, he'd have picked someone
else other than Chester to lean on, if he'd been left
alone. He didn't like the looks of the tall hawkeyed
man. There was something about him, a coldness that
could be felt, that signaled a deadly man. But Jug
didn't fear him; he'd just have rather picked someone
easier to lean on. Oh well, he told himself, the man
seemed glad that Raymond had intervened, so more
than likely the man was scared. Jug was used to people being afraid of him, and in Chester's silence, he
read fear. If the man feared him, that fight was
halfway won.

"I'm sorry about that," Raymond said quietly as
Chester sat back down.

"You're sorry for what?" Chester asked just as quietly. "I don't remember you doing anything but saving a fool a whole lot of trouble."

Raymond grinned, "Yeah, I'd bet money he'd get
more than he bargained for."

Both men laughed "I'm due in court this week, so
I don't want any trouble if I can avoid it. So thanks
for what you did, Ray."

The sound of the outer door opening brought the
men to attention. "I hope that's my bondsman,"
Raymond said quickly.

"It's more than likely the men coming back from
court. My partner, Willie, went over to get sentenced

today, Ray. I hope he came out okay."

Before Ray could reply, the men were there. The inmates stood in front of the door, waiting to be let in. "What is it? What is it?" Willie yelled from outside the bars. He was grinning widely.

"Goddamn, baby boy!" Chester yelled back. "For a man who just got sentenced, you sure seem happy."

"That's right, Chester, I know I'll be on my way to prison and out of this funky motherfucker sometime this week."

"Where's Tony at? They still keeping him downstairs?" Chester inquired as the turnkey opened the door and the men came in.

"Shit! Tony done played his way out of this shit," Willie exclaimed as he came over and sat down on the bunk. Chester introduced him to Raymond, then Willie continued, "Tony played it to the bone, baby. They gave him five years probation." Willie reached into his pocket and pulled out two dollars. "Here's part of the money he owed you. He said he'd send the rest up, plus you can have all that shit under his bunk.

"Hey, motherfucker!" Willie yelled as one of the white boys that had gone to court with him began removing the stuff from under Tony's bunk. "Bring all that shit right over here—that goes for the books, too."

As the man brought the few candy bars and books over, Chester asked, "Well, what about you? It's for damn sure you didn't get probation, but it must not have been too bad, judging from the way you've been grinning."

"That's right. The great white father didn't give me but three to twenty. Can you dig it? Three to twenty. Shit! I'll be going before the parole board in twenty-four months. I'll be on the streets, year after next, man."

"Yeah, but Tony's on the goddamn streets already," Chester said coldly. "That shows you how fucked up this system is. If anybody should have got probation, it should have been you."

Willie shrugged. "I care, man, but ain't no sense me crying about it. I'm happy I got the time I got. So Tony got out today, well, he was lookin' for it, but I wasn't. I was lookin' for something like ten to twenty. If I hadn't come up right behind Tony, I doubt if I would have got the play that I got. As it was, since the judge had given the white boy probation for the same charge, he didn't want it to look too bad by loading me down, so he gave me a break. And don't forget, Chester, Tony had money behind him. I had a fuckin' public defender fighting my case, so I'm considering myself lucky, can you dig it?"

Chester grinned. "I goddamn sure can dig it, Willie, and I don't want to seem like I don't appreciate your getting such a small menial sentence. But man, I can't help wishing you could have got the same fuckin' play that Tony got. I just can't help it. I know you should have walked if he did."

Raymond glanced from one man to the next, bewildered, until Chester explained it to him. Raymond cursed. "Ain't that a bitch! The honkie had gunplay in his case, too." He shook his head. "You can't beat these 'woods, no matter how you try. If they don't get you out on the streets, they'll end up fuckin' you when they get you in the courtrooms. Maybe now you'll understand a little better why I'm selling my house without ever stepping back into it again."

"I understood that from the bell. It's just sickening that it happens this way, that's all."

The doors opened again, and the turnkey came strolling back. He stopped in front of their ward. "Raymond Wilson? Get your stuff, you're on your way home."

Raymond grinned, pulled his smokes out and gave them to Chester. He reached in his pocket and removed ten dollars. "I hope this will help you, Chester," he said. "I'll try and come down to court the morning you go." He leaned over and shook Willie's hand. "Take care, my man," he said and headed for the door.

Jug rushed up to him as he was leaving. If Jug hadn't got in his way, Raymond wouldn't even have spoken. "Say, Ray baby, how about mashing some dough on me before you go. You know, enough to keep me in smokes."

"I'm sorry, Jug, I just gave my man all that I could spare."

"Come on if you're coming," the guard yelled. Raymond continued on towards the door, oblivious to the murderous look that Jug threw his way.

"You sure came down on me shitty," Jug yelled at his departing back.

When Raymond reached the open door and stepped through, he turned around and stared at Jug. "Man, I don't know where you're coming from. I don't owe you nothing and I ain't never promised you nothing, so what the hell is your problem?"

Jug managed to control his temper. "I wanted to really ask you if you'd go the hundred dollar bill it takes to raise me, man. I'd lay it back on you. You know a hundred dollars ain't nothing."

"I realize that, Jug, but I might as well fact with you. If it took five dollars to get you out, I wouldn't put it up, man." Ray's eyes had a bleak look to them. "We live in different worlds, Jug, altogether different."

Jug glared angrily. "You better believe we do and hope when I get out we don't run into each other." As Raymond started to walk away, Jug added, "That's why the police slapped your son, man. Your son is a gumpy, a punk, just like his daddy." As Raymond continued to walk, without looking back, Jug shouted, "It's a good thing you got out, punk, cause if you hadn't, I would've put some dick in your faggot ass tonight, you punk motherfucker!"

His voice rang up and down the corridor. Men in the other wards laughed loudly at Raymond's expense, but it didn't make any difference. Raymond knew that he was on his way home, and no matter what an ignorant bastard said or how many people laughed, he was free again. And if things went right, he planned to remain free.

12

IT WAS CHESTER'S MORNING for court and he was damn glad of it. Since Jug's arrival on the ward, everything had reverted to the law of the survival of the fittest. Jug hadn't wasted any time trying to take over. He took food from the weak, anyone who he thought might be afraid of him—black or white—and he'd started raping the weaker men.

A young, thin, light-complexioned homosexual had been put on the ward, and Jug almost went out of his mind. He appeared to be completely in love. He couldn't stand for any of the other black or white men on the ward to even speak to the young man. With the help of the homosexual, Jug had turned out a young white boy by the name of Jerry. In the evenings, Jug had to make it a point to get enough meat off the other men's trays to support his stable.

There were only a few men in the ward who were immune. Chester and Willie stuck so close together that Jug realized that, if he even attempted to take food from one of them, he'd have both of them to contend with. He was biding his time, though. He knew that any day now, Willie would be called out to go to Jackson Prison, then he planned on bringing the arrogant Chester down to his knees.

The turnkey came down the rock calling out the names of the men due in court that morning. "David Walker, Chester Hines, Jean Jackson. You guys ready?" The last name he called, Jean Jackson, was the light-complexioned homosexual.

As the guard went on down the corridor, Jug pulled Jean close and embraced him, the same way a man would a woman. They stood toe to toe, kissing. Chester almost became overcome with disgust. He wasn't sick to his stomach; he had witnessed this same kind of scene many times before in the joint. It was a common sight in prison, seeing two men kissing. What really disturbed Chester was his total dislike for the man called Jug. The man's nugatory notoriety and his actions were sickening enough, without any extra display of his depravity.

Chester drew a breath of relief when the guard came back and let them out. He waved at Willie and followed the rest of the men down the catwalk. Idly, Chester wondered if something was wrong with his mind. Simple things seemed to get on his nerves lately. What it all boiled down to, he told himself, was the fact that he was going to have to lock ass with the big bully. The sooner it happened, the better off he'd be, he believed. As things stood, his nerves were getting worse and worse, waiting for the moment when the fight would jump off. He realized what the hold-up was all about. Jug was scared to do anything at the present time because of Willie. As soon as Willie shipped out though, the shit would hit the fan. The big bastard was just waiting. But what Jug didn't realize was that Chester was just waiting too. He believed in his heart he could take the large man. All that fat around his stomach was testimony to the fact that Jug had a weakness. Also, Chester figured, the man's nightly sex parties with Jerry and Jean had to leave him weak, to some extent.

On the elevator down, Jean moved over near Chester and attempted to start up a conversation. "Hi, Chester," he began, glancing down at the floor shyly, as a bashful woman would do. "You seem to go out of your way to ignore me; I mean, you're not frightened by Jug, I can tell that just from looking at you."

Chester glared down at the homosexual. "No, baby," he said, "I don't go out of my way to ignore you, but since I don't use, I don't see any reason for us to have any drawn-out conversations, since all that they'd do would be to cause trouble between me and your man."

"Well, I guess you know you're not going to be able to get around trouble with my man. You know, all he's really waiting on is for your friend to ship out to Jackson. He's told me so many times, Chester, what's going to happen to you as soon as Willie leaves, that it's become sickening. You know, like a record you hear over and over again. I'm tired of hearing what all he's going to do to you."

Chester tried to grin. There it was out in the open. He had thought that was what the reason was; now he knew for sure. The best thing he could do would be to get together with Willie and kick the shit out of Jug tonight, to get it over with while he held the winning hand.

As the elevator came to a halt, Jean turned around and leaned heavy against Chester, pushing his bony buttocks up against Chester's penis. Some of the other inmates on the elevator grinned as they noticed the action.

Chester pushed him roughly away. "Keep your filthy ass off me, boy. I told you I don't use! I don't fuck with punks. Now, can you understand that, *man*?" Chester stated loudly, drawing out the word man.

Jean tossed his head back. "Well!" he exclaimed loudly, "I guess I know when I'm not wanted. But I've got a friend who might not like it if I was to tell him the way a certain person treated me."

All at once anger overcame reason. Chester reached out and grabbed the homosexual roughly. "Listen, punk, and you better listen close. I don't have time for games, boy. I'm going to court fighting for my freedom, and here you are fucking around with some bullshit. Now I'm going to tell you something, kid, and you better pay heed. I've seen too many men die because of punks like you, so if anything should jump off in my direction because of something you've said, I'll personally kick sparks out of your motherfuckin' sorry ass!"

"Okay you guys, let's cut that shit off back there," a guard said from the front of the elevator. The men slowly got out and played follow-the-leader. Before they were taken across the street, they were handcuffed tightly together.

David made it a point to get close to Chester. "That bitch ain't nothing but trouble," he stated as they started walking across the street.

Chester stared straight ahead, ignoring the man's words. He was still too angry to control his voice. He counted the bobbing heads in front of him. There were twenty men handcuffed in his group. Behind them another group of handcuffed men followed. When they reached the steps, Chester glanced back and he could see two more groups of prisoners coming across the street. Guards stood out in the middle of the street, carrying riot guns and shotguns.

"I'll just be glad when this shit is over with," he said softly, not really speaking to anyone in particular.

"Know just what you mean, Chester," David replied quickly. He welcomed conversation, anything to take his mind off of what lay ahead.

"I talked to my damn lawyer, a public defender at that," David began, "and the bastard asked me if I wanted to cop out to a lesser charge. I told that motherfucker I wouldn't cop out to a ten-day offense. I ain't did a motherfuckin' thing, so I ain't pleading guilty to nothing." Once he began speaking it was like a damn opening; he couldn't seem to stop. "Hell no, I ain't accepting no cop-out. These motherfuckers got me charged with a rape case, yet I ain't raped nobody. I'm demanding a jury trial, just like you told me to do. Yes sir, it's going to go before the people so that they can see just how these bastards try and fuck over a man."

"Okay, you guys, hold it down back there," a guard said as he walked up and down the line. A young white woman, an office worker, came out of a side room. As soon as she saw the line of men, she started to go back inside the office she came out of, but then changed her mind and came hurrying past, clutching some papers to her well-developed bosom. The small mini-skirt she wore flopped up between her legs with each giant step she took.

"Goddamn," one of the men in the rear yelled, "look at all that white pussy. I bet that bitch can ride a dick!"

From the way the girl's ears became red, the men closest to her could tell that she had heard. She almost broke out and ran then, to get away from the line of prisoners.

A white guard, his face flushed red with anger, ran up and down the line searching for the man who had yelled out. "I wish I knew which one of you bastards said that," he stated, and there was no doubting that if he found out, it would go awfully hard on the man.

"You uncouth sonofabitches!" the guard cursed under his breath but loud enough for some of the men to hear him.

David started to go back to their conversation again but Chester cut him off. "Quiet, man. The fuckin' guard's already mad as hell. If he catches you running your mouth, you might end up in the hole tonight." Chester didn't really believe what he said, but he didn't want to listen; he was preoccupied with his own thoughts. It was enough to listen every night to the men cry about their cases, but now that he was on his way to court, he wanted time to collect his own thoughts.

The guard put the men in bull pens. They sat there from early morning until the judges finally came to work, which was never before nine o'clock. The judges had their coffee breaks first, then the prisoners were led into the courtrooms where they stood handcuffed until it was near time for them to appear before the bench. Then, and only then, a guard removed the handcuffs. By the time Chester was ready to go before the judge, he had made up his mind to what he would do.

"Chester Hines?"

His name was called out and he stepped lightly up to stand in front of the judge.

"How do you plead at this time?" he was asked.

"Your honor, I've been in the county jail for damn near six months now," Chester said. "I'd like to plead guilty and ask the court to pass sentence on me today please."

The white-haired judge glanced down at him briefly, then shuffled some papers in front of him. "From your past record, Mister Hines, it doesn't seem as though you have learned anything. Since you've asked me to pass sentence today, I'll do just that. You've entered a plea of guilty, so the court now sentences you to three-and-a-half years to four. You may have the time already spent in the county jail as time already served," the judge stated gravely, as if he were really giving away something.

"Thanks for nothing, whitey!" Chester replied loudly as a guard ran up to him. Chester knew as well as the judge did that the time served in the county jail was automatic. They had to give it to you, even if they didn't want to.

As Chester was led away he stared at the long line of black men waiting to step in front of the machine-like judge. They weren't even faces to the judge; they were just black shadows that passed his way every day, shadows with folders on them, telling what they had done in the past and where they should be put in the future. What most of the men didn't know was that the judge had read their records and written down on the folder while he was at home that past evening, sipping scotch, just how much time to give the man whose folder he held. Each folder had a certain amount of years written out on it; very seldom was there an exception.

Appearing in court was just the whitewash. The case had been settled long before the prisoner got up and ate his morning breakfast, Chester thought.

David rushed up to the bars when Chester reentered the bull pen. "How did you make out, brother?"

"The motherfucker gave me three-and-a-half to four," Chester replied, not showing emotion of any kind. There was nothing left. He hadn't expected anything other than what he got. He had hoped for a slightly lighter sentence, one that left room for parole, but it didn't make that much difference. That's why he hadn't bothered to tell his wife that he was due in court that morning. He didn't want to see any tears, didn't want to show any emotion. All he wanted to do was get to prison and start doing his time. Once he got to prison, he could start living like a human being again. He'd have clean sheets on his bed once a week, clean clothes to wear, clean toilets to use, privacy for a change. Yes, he'd be damn glad to get to prison.

Chester glanced up and saw the sneer on the homosexual Jean's face. The punk enjoyed the thought of his having received some time, Chester thought. Just for the hell of it, Chester walked over and stared down at the punk. "What's wrong, Jean, you afraid to laugh? You look like you're about to bust from trying to hold back that grin. Go ahead. Enjoy yourself."

Jean put his hands on his hips. "I couldn't care less about how much time you got," he said. "I only wish I could have been in the judge's place for a few minutes. I'd have given you life!"

The slap came instantly. As Jean's head snapped back, Chester followed it up with another one. They were vicious, brutal slaps, and the sound was still ringing in everyone's ears when Chester slapped him again. Tears sprang from Jean's eyes. "Try laughing that one off, punk!" Chester said. "Now you got something to go running to your man with. That saves you the trouble of thinking up a lie. Also, it will give you a better reason to wish I got life." With that, Chester slapped him again and then walked away.

Jean sat on the bench and cried like a little girl. When the guard opened the door to let another man in, Jean ran up to the bars screaming, "He hit me, he hit me!"

The guard glanced at the homosexual, then slammed the door in his face. "Try acting like a man for a change," the guard said as he locked the door. The men inside the bull pen laughed loudly. Now that Jean had shown that he was a snitch, they didn't have any pity for him.

"David Walker, David Walker, are you back there?" a red-faced, blond-headed man yelled from the front of the bull pen.

Chester watched David coldly as the young man stood at the bars arguing with his lawyer. He kept shaking his head stubbornly, then he roared, "I don't give a fuck what you say, man! I want a jury trial, and I ain't pleading guilty to nothing!"

The lawyer continued to argue, but it was useless. David continued shaking his head. Finally he turned his back on the lawyer and walked away from the steel door. He stopped in front of Chester. "That motherfucker is crazy if he thinks I'm going to plead guilty to attempted rape!"

For the first time since appearing in front of the judge, Chester grinned. "That's it, blood, stick with it, man. Don't let them motherfuckers talk you into accepting no goddamn cop-out—not if it happened like you said. You'd be crazy as hell to plead guilty to anything if you didn't do nothing. Tell that red-faced motherfucker when he comes back that you'll plead guilty to being drunk, if he can get it broke down to drunk sleeping, but that's about the only thing you'll accept."

David shook his head in agreement. "You're damn right, man. I ain't coppin' out to a fuckin' thing! I ain't did nothing."

The turnkey came back and called out David's name. He walked out of the bull pen as though he were going to his death. In about three minutes he was back. He had stuck to his guns and pleaded not guilty, then requested a jury trial. The judge had appeared angry, but since the man refused anything but a jury trial, he was going to get it.

"It will take a while for them to try your case, David, but I wish you all the luck in the world," Chester said seriously. "You stick with it, man, and try and make that fuckin' lawyer of yours get some black faces on your jury. You're going to need everything you can get to come from under this, blood."

"I know, man, I damn well know. I just wish I could afford a damn lawyer. My rap partner is testifying that I didn't have anything to do with it, so I know I should walk."

"Well, just have patience, blood, and everything

might work out. It's going to take a little time, but I
believe you have a good case, especially if your rap
partner takes the stand in your behalf. I don't see how
they can find you guilty of anything," Chester said to
him quietly. "Just keep the faith, baby."

The turnkey arrived and started calling the names
of those who had been to court. Chester and David
lined up at the door. As soon as their names were
called, they went out together.

Jean yelled after them. "You better have them put
you in another ward, 'cause when I get there, I'm sure
going to tell Jug what you did."

Chester didn't even bother to look back. He
answered Jean sharply, "You better get ready for a
good ass-kickin' then, 'cause when we get finished
with Jug, I'm going to stick a broomstick straight up
your ass. So you just come on with it when you get
back."

The same procedure was followed as they went
back across the street. Guards lined up in the middle
of the street, guns at the ready. They were stuck in a
bull pen until the rest of the men they had left in the
courtroom bull pens caught up with them. Jean came
in, glancing around nervously, then walked over to
where Chester sat.

"Man, I don't know what got into me earlier today,
Chester, but I'm sorry. If you want to, we can forget
about what happened today. I won't say anything if
you don't, okay?"

"That's all right with me," Chester replied. It was
a relief off his mind. He hadn't really wanted any trou-

ble. He had slapped Jean without thought. It was something he rarely did—put his hands on another man, or woman for that matter. As he grew older, his dislike for violence had grown. He had come in touch with so much violence in his youth that he now detested it. Only when money was involved was he able to resort to it without any emotion; then he was a deadly weapon, capable of anything.

He held out his hand to Jean. "How about it, Jean, will you accept my apology? I was upset over the time I'd got, baby, you know how it is."

Jean smiled and held his hand longer than necessary. "That's all right, Chester; you know I like a man who's strong. Maybe we can get together when I get to Jackson, humm?"

The sound of the dinner wagon came to them. It was that time. In minutes they would be on their way back upstairs. Some of the men in the lock-up would stay up there until after Christmas before they'd get a chance to come downstairs again. The women prisoners were let out first. Chester found himself rushing to the front of the cell so that he could get a look at the young girls in their mini-skirts. It had been quite a while since he'd seen a woman.

13

THE MEN IN CHESTER'S ward were celebrating. In the morning quite a few of them were shipping out to Jackson. The rumor floating around the county jail was that there were so many men going out that they were using a bus to take the load of men up, instead of the state cars that they ordinarily used.

Chester had spent all of the loose cigarettes he had for some spud juice. Willie, following Chester's lead, did the same thing. They had three quarts of the homemade juice.

"Say, Chester," Jug said, approaching Chester's bunk, "how about selling me one of them bottles, my man?" His voice was mild; it was seldom that he used that tone, except when he wanted a favor.

Slowly Chester lit a cigarette. He was in a jocular mood. He didn't know for sure, but he believed he was on the shipment in the morning, too. It was supposed to be a large one. If so, he and Willie would make the trip to Jackson together. From the rumors that were flying back and forth between the wards, it was said that there would be two trips made, one in the morning and one when the bus got back in the afternoon. Either way, he was sure he'd make one of them, if the rumor was true.

"Okay, Jug, I'll let you have one. How much are you willing to pay for it?"

Jug made a gesture with his hands. "I mean, brother, you know, I ain't handling the way you and Willie are, but I'll spend as much as I can for it."

"How much is as much as you can?" Willie asked quickly from his position on the bunk.

"I might be able to raise, say, five packs of smokes?"

Willie shook his head. "Man, we don't need no smokes. We can't take them with us, so cigarettes won't do us no good. We have got to have cash money, my man, cash money."

"What about two dollars?" Jug asked slowly, his eyes beginning to turn mean.

Willie laughed in his face. "You got to be joking, Jug. You know how much that shit cost us? If you don't, I'll give you the information. Them there little old quarts cost us a carton of smokes apiece, so the least we can take is…." He hesitated briefly, as if adding something up in his mind, then stated, "three dollars and fifty cents."

Jug turned to Chester for support. "Man, I ain't got that much paper. How about giving me a little play? I'll tell you what, I'll have my ladies put on a show for everybody, if you guys decide to give me a little play." Jug said it loudly, for everybody's benefit. "How about it, Chester? I'll lay two bucks on you and give you ringside seats for my show."

"For a guy pimpin' like you're doing, Jug, I don't see how one dollar should make any difference to your bankroll," Willie replied just as loud, so that everybody could hear.

This time Jug gave him a look that was full of hate and contempt. "Whose shit is it, man? Yours or Chester's?" he said, the anger in his voice coming out.

"The dollar don't make that much difference," Chester said, intervening. "I'm not interested in no damn show, though. The stuff belongs to both of us, Jug, so whatever Willie says goes. As far as I'm concerned, since I'm leaving in the morning, you can have the shit for two dollars, but it's still up to Willie."

Willie glanced at his partner. "You know we'll be losing bread if we let it go for less than we paid for it, Chester." Jug started to say something, but Willie waved him silent. "But if you don't really care, it's cool with me, too." As soon as he finished talking, he reached under the bed and removed a bottle that they had been drinking out of.

"Where's the money?" Willie said, holding the spud juice in his hand. He waited until Jug had paid him, then he tossed one of the dollars over to Chester and put the other one in his pocket. "Oh yeah, I'll be at ringside for the floor show, Jug," he said harshly, not bothering to keep the contempt out of his voice.

Jug glanced at the bottle. "Why I got to get the bottle that's been drank out of?" he asked sharply, turning the bottle around in his hands.

"Well, we ain't got no other ones for sale. Either you accept that one or none at all. It don't make no goddamn difference to me what you do," Willie said coldly. The animosity between the two men couldn't be hidden. For some reason, Jug had taken a personal dislike to Willie that surpassed his hatred for Chester.

"Fuck it! If you want to be petty about it, motherfuck it!" Jug exclaimed hotly; his little pig-like eyes glittered dangerously. "When I get to Jackson, Willie, maybe you and I can kick this shit around again." The threat was open and Willie didn't back up.

"Man, you ain't got to wait until you get to Jackson to do nothing, Jug! If you got a problem, man, you can get it off your chest right now. It don't make me no kind of difference, can you dig it?"

"Aw, man," Chester said quietly, "why don't you guys be cool. We riding out of here in the morning, Willie, so why get involved. This time tomorrow night, we'll be laying up in our own private cells with the earphones on listening to some smokin' jazz on the box." Chester twisted around on his bunk and took a long swig out of the quart of spud juice he had. "You got your bottle of juice, man, so why don't you pull on up, Jug? Ain't no sense in you guys getting uptight over nothing, man. I'm in too good a mood. Go get your bitches drunk, maybe they'll put on a good show then."

It was an order to move on. Jug didn't like it, but he really couldn't do anything else about it. To fight one was to fight both of them. He hoped that in the morning they would just call out one of them, leaving the other one. Then he'd make that cocksucker pay, he'd bet money on it. By the time he got finished kicking whichever one was left in the ass, he'd more than make up for the shitty way they came down on him.

"Yeah, man, I'll ride out. I think this is the second time you done asked me away from your bunk, my man. I hope there ain't no reason for it to happen a third time, Chester," Jug stated; his voice had taken on a deep bass in his anger. He strutted away, waving to his two homosexuals to join him. Jug stretched out on his bunk, lying on his back. Jerry climbed in beside him. The two men lay side by side kissing, until the sound of the turnkey making his nightly rounds came to them. Jerry got up and stood beside the bed; Jean sat on the floor. After the guard left, Jean beat Jerry back into Jug's bunk. The men lay in each other's arms, kissing, while Jug ran his hand down in Jean's pants. He worked the punk's pants down until they were around his hips.

Willie grinned as he watched the homosexuals. "Man, now that's what I call making love. If I had that much patience with my old lady in the streets,

I'd more than likely be a pimp by now."

Chester took a swig from his bottle. "I don't like to see it. It's sickening to me. How the hell he can stand to kiss them punks in the mouth is beyond me. They'll suck a dog's dick, yet he kisses them as if they were real women." Chester finished off his quart bottle. "You know, this is pretty nice spud juice," he said.

"I'll agree with you on that," Willie said as he turned up his bottle. He held the rest of it out to his friend. "Here, man, help me kill this shit. I can't drink it the way you do. I'm loaded off the small amount of shit I've drank already."

Across the way, Jug shared his drinks with his two gay boys. They drank up the remainder of the juice he had in the bottle. All the time they were drinking, Jug kept his hand on Jean's ass. It was as though he was dealing with a real woman. He glanced around casually to see who was watching, then slowly kissed Jean—a long, drawn-out kiss.

"I'm going to let my ladies put on a show for you sorry-ass motherfuckers," Jug stated loudly as he got up off his bunk. He removed a blanket and carried it to the middle of the floor. He beckoned to Jerry. "So read this out on the floor, honey," he said as he pinched Jerry's cheek.

The young white boy rushed to do what he had been requested to do. "Okay, daddy," he replied in his best female voice. As Jerry straightened out the blanket, Jug and Jean started undressing.

Jean took his portable radio and set it on the edge

of the blanket, then he found the music he wanted and started to do a strip to the music. He danced slowly, taking off his clothes to what he thought was the beat of the music. The card-playing inmates stopped long enough to watch. This was something different, something out of the ordinary. Jerry, not wanting to be outdone, got up and started to take off his clothes too. Since he couldn't really dance, he didn't make a big production out of it. He slipped out of his clothes, leaving only his shorts on.

Jug, by this time, had removed his clothes. By the time he walked over to the blanket buck-naked, Jean had finished his dance and was out of all his clothes. "Give Jerry some cap," he ordered harshly.

Jerry grinned and removed his shorts. He opened his legs and held Jean's head as the light-skinned homosexual began oral copulation on him. "Oh, yes," Jerry said loudly, "that's it! Suck it now. Don't bite, just suck it!" he directed.

As Jean followed the direction to the best of his ability, Jug got behind him and inserted his long, black penis in Jean's ass. Jean moaned but continued his lip service to Jerry.

"Man," Willie exclaimed as he watched. "I'd say that was some show they're putting on. You know, Chester, I've heard about freak parties, but this is the closest I've ever come to seeing one. It's a damn shame it had to happen while I was in jail."

Chester grinned and put down the book he had started to read. "You can probably join them without anyone complaining, Willie. Then you'd sho'nuff have something to tell the folks back home whenever you got there."

"No way! I think I'll pass on that!" Willie replied, then added, "But an old vet like you, Chester, that's right down your line. I'll bet you've had a lot of punk pussy in your visits inside these cherished walls."

Chester laughed deeply, the sound ringing off the walls. "You might not believe this, Willie, but I don't use. I've never had anything to do sexually with another man in my life, so I guess you might call me square."

The sound of Chester's laughter angered Jug. He imagined that Chester was laughing at his ladies and what they were doing. Here he was going out of his way to put on a show for them, and then this bastard laughed at it. It really angered him. Jug decided to do something that would take the laughter out of it.

He removed his penis from Jean's ass, "You just keep on sucking that bone, girl," he instructed as he walked over to his bunk. He glanced back to make sure that Jean was following his orders. The freak show was still going on. Jerry was enjoying himself too well to reach a climax. He was still giving out emotional orders.

Jug removed a cylindrical shaped candy bar from his belongings. As he walked back towards the freaking-off couple, he slowly removed the wrapper. He grinned at Chester and Willie, who were watching him curiously. There was no humor in his smile; his eyes were cold and ruthless.

"I hope all this ain't boring you guys," he said coldly. Everybody in the ward knew that he was speaking to Chester and Willie, even though he didn't mention names.

When he reached the blanket, he bent down and spread the cheeks of Jean's ass. He slowly pushed the candy bar up into the man's rectum, then he pulled him off of Jerry and made him lie on his stomach. He pointed at the candy bar, "I want you to get it, get every motherfuckin' crumb of that good candy bar," he said to Jerry.

Jerry stared at him dumbfounded. Jug reached over and slapped him viciously across the mouth. "I said I want you to eat that candy bar out of his ass!" he ordered. There was no doubt in his voice; Jerry knew at once that Jug meant just what he said.

Again Jerry hesitated, but another slap across the face started him off. "Please, Jug," he begged, "not that. I'll do anything but that!"

"You'll do that, punk, and you'll do it now!" Jug ordered sharply. "I don't want to tell you again. Now take care of business."

"Come on, honey," Jean begged, "that stuff feels funny up inside of me. Hurry up, Jerry."

Jerry glanced up at Jug one more time, then dropped his head and started to give Jean a rim job.

"You still like freak shows?" Chester asked Willie, as he noticed the strange color that was coming into Willie's face.

Willie looked as though he was about to throw up.

"Man," he said, "he'd have to kill me. I mean, man, I'd die and go to hell before I'd allow somebody to make me do some crazy shit like that." He watched the freak show as though hypnotized. He couldn't take his eyes from it. He shook his head. "Any mother-fucker low enough to make another man do something like that against his will should be dead! He's a lowlife motherfucker, and his mammy should have crossed her legs when she had him," Willie said, and his voice was nowhere near low.

Whether Jug heard him or not, he didn't let on. Maybe in his heart he knew he had gone too far. Something must have warned him, because if he had said anything out of the ordinary to Willie or Chester, he would have had to prove his manhood.

14

WHEN DAWN BROKE and a ray of light came through the windows high up on the outside of the bars, Chester rolled over and lit another cigarette. He had been thinking about what had happened that past evening; now he couldn't wait until the turnkey came by, calling out the names of the men shipping out that morning. He had had enough. If he stayed on the ward any longer he'd more than likely end up killing Jug. He knew it; it was a fact. He was too well aware of himself. He thought the man was an animal, unfit to live beside other men.

"What are you trying to do, smoke up all your cigarettes before you leave today?" Willie asked from the other bunk.

"You better believe it," Chester replied. He smiled in the semi-darkness. His friendship with Willie had really grown. He had met many men in prison, made many acquaintances, but never before had he allowed himself to become so close to another man. In reality, even though Chester hated to admit it to himself, Willie was really the first man he had ever been able to call friend. Chester was a loner, so it came as a surprise to him that he had allowed a man to get that close.

"Well, buddy," Willie said, "it won't be long now. In a little while we'll know."

Each man fell silent, each drifted with his own private thoughts. Each man was well aware that, if they didn't go together, he'd have a hell of a fight on his hands. But neither man seemed too worried about it. The lights on the catwalk went on, and the coffee wagon appeared. As soon as the chow wagon was past, a turnkey showed up calling names.

The guard started at the last ward in the rear, then worked his way back. When he reached ward two, the first name he called was Willie's. Chester waited, damn near sure he would be disappointed, then the guard called his name. "You guys got fifteen minutes to get ready," he roared, then went on down the rock.

The two friends glanced at each other. They grinned, then rushed to get ready. Actually there was nothing to take, since they both knew they couldn't even take a pack of new cigarettes inside the prison. They said their goodbyes quickly. It was all over that soon. It seemed like seconds before the guard was back, opening the door and calling out to the men, "The Jackson express is awaiting!"

Most of the prisoners who came out of the wards seemed happy to be going. They grinned at each other, joked with men in the other wards. All of them had something in common: they were either smiling or laughing loudly. A passerby who didn't know would have thought the men were going home. He would never guess that they were all on their way to the state prison. But that was the way the county jail affected a man. After staying there any length of time, the men were glad to go to prison, just to get away from the sorry food, the sorry sleeping conditions, the unwholesome closeness of a lot of men shoved inside a small ward with nothing to occupy their minds.

The men went down in the elevator. Once they reached the basement floor, they were handcuffed, three men to each file. There were twelve men handcuffed altogether. Chester counted them, then recounted them. It didn't seem like enough men for a bus, he reasoned. Six sheriff's deputies were waiting for the handcuffed men. They escorted them out three at a time. Waiting for them outside were two station wagons. The men were put in, then their feet were shackled together.

"You guys can smoke," one of the deputies said, as he finished shackling the men's feet. Two more deputies brought out another three men and they were put in the last row of seats in the station wagon. There was a strong wire screen separating the men from the occupants in the driver's seat. Three deputies climbed inside the station wagon that held Chester and Willie.

The ride to Jackson was quick; it took less than three hours, and most of it was on the expressway. The deputies didn't worry about breaking any speed laws. They drove as fast as they wanted. The prisoners joked back and forth with the guards. The guards had been on their jobs so long it was nothing new to them to see happy men on their way to prison. They never got any further than the basement, where they picked up their prisoners, but they had escorted so many men to prison that they knew beyond a shadow of a doubt that something was wrong with the county jail. Anything that would make a man look forward to reaching the bleak walls of Jackson Prison must be a hell hole.

Finally they turned off the highway, with the other station wagon right behind them, and turned in at the prison gates. The men inside the station wagon who had never seen the prison before stared at it in wonder. It was the largest prison in the country, and from the outside it looked it.

The guard at the gate waved them straight through. They drove down a well-paved street. Trusties were everywhere; some were picking up paper. They were all well dressed, in clean blue outfits, with matching jackets for those who bothered to wear jackets on the warm, sunny day. The men looked well fed; they glanced idly at the station wagon as it went past. Some of them waved; they knew that here was a load of men headed for quarantine.

The station wagon which held Chester and Willie pulled up in front of a large red building. "Well, this is it," Chester said, not speaking to anyone in particular.

The deputies led the men inside the building. As soon as they entered, the deputies began taking off the shackles. "Well, boys," the deputy said good-naturedly," looks like you've found yourselves a new home."

As soon as the shackles were off, the deputy pointed to another room, which had a bench running along the entire wall. "In there," he directed.

The prisoners lined up outside the door they were directed to enter. They had to wait until a guard inside a bulletproof control room pushed a button, then the door quietly opened. As soon as the men entered, a prison trusty was waiting for them.

"You guys take your clothes off," the trusty said. "If you want to send them home, fill out one of these cards; if you want to give them to the Red Cross, just put them in that big container. When I call your name, go in there and get under the shower. Don't come out until another inmate shows you which way to go. There's soap on the shelves against the wall. Put the soap back when you finish, and keep the noise down."

Some of the men who had never been in prison before stared at the prisoner closely. They couldn't tell if he was a guard or prisoner. Some of them called him "sir," and others used the term "officer." He quickly corrected the first man who called him an officer. "Listen, mac," the middle-aged colored trusty said, "I'm a con just like you, so knock off that offi-

cer shit. Call me any motherfucker fuckin' thing but
that!"

The man who was corrected stared at him in wonder. The trusty was dressed in street clothes: black
pants, a pretty turtleneck shirt, blue in color, and he
wore expensive shoes.

Chester grinned as he stepped up to the desk; he
spoke to the trusty, "What's happenin', John, these
honkies ain't let you out yet?"

The trusty glanced up, then smiled, "What's going
on, Chest? You couldn't stay out there where it's nice
at, huh? How much did you bring with you this time?"

"Three-and-a-half to four," Chester said quietly as
he gripped the older man's hand.

"Shit!" John exclaimed. "You ain't got nothing but
a wake-up. You can do that shit on top of your head,
man. Your dick won't even be done got hard before
it'll be time for you to go to dress out." He pointed
his finger towards the shower, "When you finish in
there, you tell that goddamn barber that I said you're
a personal friend of mine and to look out for you. Tell
him I said I'll give him a pack of smokes when I finish up in here."

Chester grinned, shook the man's hand, then
removed all his clothes. All the men had to leave
everything they owned on top of the desk where John
sat. The lone guard in the reception room with him
didn't even bother to take his head out of the paper-
back he was reading.

Inside the shower room, Chester enjoyed himself,
feeling clean for the first time in months. He listened

as two new men spoke of the inmate, about how they'd never have guessed that he was a prisoner. "Damn," one of them exclaimed, "did you see that fuckin' watch he had on? Shit, it must have cost four or five hundred."

Chester didn't bother to tell him that it probably came out of some fool's property, someone fool enough to wear an expensive watch like that up to the prison. A man could take a watch in, but he had to swear it didn't cost over fifty dollars. If it cost more, it went into his property bag or he sent it home. Either way, it had to go through too many hands—prisoner hands at that—for it to ever reach its destination.

Another trusty entered the shower carrying something that looked like a fire-extinguisher, but it was a device containing chemicals to kill lice and other things like crabs that men carried coming out of the county jail. As each man left the shower, he was sprayed good, then he stepped into another shower in the next room. Here an officer waited, where the man had to bend over and spread his cheeks. His hair was felt, ears were looked in—not a spot was missed. They tried to make sure that no contraband was brought in. The men were led buck naked through this room, then to the next, where they were issued a white uniform to put on, with slippers. This would be their outfit until the next day, when they would be given brand new clothes that fit, including a new pair of shoes and one pair of boots for working. Shorts, tee-shirts, everything had their prison number stamped inside them.

The haircut was a joke; the barber cut an inmate's hair in less than three minutes. Chester told the white inmate barber what John had said. The barber took five minutes on his head. He glanced in the mirror. It was better than that given to the rest of the men.

Willie joined him on the bench, dressed in his white outfit, sporting his new haircut, where they waited to go before a trusty and fill out the papers with the information that the prison demanded. Pictures were taken, fingerprints, and so on. After what seemed like hours of waiting, they were finished. The men lined up and were led down a corridor, where a door was opened, leading them into the main hall of the quarantine. Benches, rows of them, were the first thing that came to view. This was where they ate, on base, and where the once-a-week movie was shown. The men were fed as much as they wanted, except for meat. They were each given just one piece of meat, but it was large. Milk was served, as much as they wanted, and the men could have as much bread as they could eat. This was a treat after months in the county jail, and the men ate like pigs.

When they finished eating, they were led down base, the first floor of the blocks. An inmate stood at an empty cell passing out bundles with blankets and sheets in them. Each man was then given a tag with a number on it, which was his cell number.

Chester glanced at his number. Fourth gallery, number 68. It figured. They put the young inmates down on base with the men who were too old to walk up the steps. The old convicts, vets, were put on the top galleries. The hacks didn't worry about them too much. Nobody in their right mind would think of raping one of them. They were generally hardened men, men who knew their way around. Since Chester had an old number, the guards knew he was an old inmate.

Willie caught up with Chester. He was on three, in number 52. The men carried their belongings and went up the stairway side by side, laughing and talking. It was a relief to be where they were. They would be in quarantine for at least a month, but it wasn't anywhere near as bad as the county jail.

15

CHESTER HAD BEEN in quarantine three weeks when David came through. He wasn't too surprised to see the man, jury trial or not. He stopped him after chow one afternoon and asked how much time he had brought.

David looked at him blankly for a minute, then remembered who he was. "Oh, hi, Chester," he said, "them motherfuckers gave me twenty to twenty-five. Years man, years! Can you imagine that? Twenty-five years for something I'm not guilty of."

Chester flinched but tried to not show it as the man walked off in a daze. After that, Chester made it a point to avoid David whenever he saw him. He mentioned it to Willie one day.

"Shit. you ain't got to avoid him. He walks around in a daze anyway. I doubt if they'll allow him to stay inside population; they'll probably send him on top of six block," Willie said.

It went that way until Chester went out to population. He left a week before Willie. They put him in three block. By the time Willie came out and was put in two block, he had his routine down pat. He worked in the kitchen, in the dishwashing room where they took care of the trays. After paying the inmate foreman two boxes of cigarettes, he was given the job of bowl man. Whenever they served a meal and didn't have bowls, Chester didn't have to work. Only in the mornings or whenever they served chili or soup. The inmate foreman took roll call and covered him; he didn't have to worry about that, either.

Frequently Chester could be found on the back yard, running. After he got his first year in on his sentence, he started running every day so that he would be in shape whenever he got out. He spent another four boxes of cigarettes to pay a prison clerk so that he wouldn't be shipped outside to one of the farms. He'd decided to do his whole bit inside the wall. Out in trusty division, a man had a chance to get his hands on reefer or heroin, but since Chester didn't shoot dope, it didn't bother him. He could buy reefer sometimes inside the wall. A stick of weed cost a man one carton of smokes.

In prison, cigarettes were money. Anything a man wanted could be bought for enough cigarettes—everything but a woman, but there the punks came into play.

Inside the prison wall, it cost two boxes of cigarettes to have a relation with a homosexual. To get a head job, it cost anywhere from one box to five. It depended on the homosexual. If he was an old, gumpty punk, it was cheaper. The younger ones cost more.

After Chester had been in population for six months, Jug came inside the wall. He was there for three months before he got killed over a homosexual. Another inmate stabbed him to death during a movie.

Willie paid out three boxes of cigarettes to get the prison clerk to transfer him over to Chester's block. After that, when there was a vacancy on the third floor and Chester locked on the third tile, in cell number 24, Willie paid out another box of smokes and moved upstairs, two cells away from Chester. The two men had become exceptionally close. Now they were never far apart. They went to chow together, the movie together and all of the stage shows—or whatever other entertainment came inside the prison. The two men did everything together. Chester taught Willie how to play chess, then took the time to teach him how to play bridge. Both the men signed up for school at night. Chester took up art, learning how to mix his paint so that he could turn out pretty good oil paintings.

Since Willie couldn't paint, he took up typing and English. He started trying to write. After awhile, he could write pretty well. He started sending out short stories to the various magazines.

Each block inside the wall held close to five hun-

dred men. Each man had a private cell. Some of the
men had desks and homemade lamps inside their cells.
Each cell had its private toilet, washbowl, and each
man had a broom and a small brush to keep his toilet clean. The cells were checked every day by the
guard on duty while the men were out on their jobs.
If a cell was found dirty, the man was given a ticket.
Too many tickets resulted in the man ending up doing
time in the prison hole.

All the while Chester was locked up, he never got
a ticket. A convict passed down the rock each morning at about six o'clock with the mop bucket. He put
the mop in a man's cell and then stood outside and
waited until the man finished mopping. Then he went
on to the next cell. This was the inmate's job. He
passed out the mop. It was considered a good job
because the man was finished working before eight
o'clock in the morning. Only on laundry day was he
called on to work later than eight o'clock. Then he
had to help pass out the men's laundry. Bedsheets
were exchanged once a week, so a man couldn't complain about having dirty sheets. All he had to do was
turn in his dirty sheets and socks and underclothes on
time each week, and he received clean ones in return.

There were two movies a week in the wintertime.
One was a pay movie, which cost twenty-five cents,
the other one, on Saturdays, was a free one for the
men who couldn't afford to pay. The jobs inside the
walls paid ten cents a day, so a man needed help from
the outside, unless he was a good gambler.

The prisoners bet on everything. Ballgames, football, basketball—no matter. When they weren't betting on the pros, they bet on the inmate games. The inmates had baseball, football, and basketball teams; they played daily. In the summer, they had night games. The men were allowed out in the yard until eight o'clock at night in the summer, then they had what you would call "night yard." Inside the wall, they had five basketball courts. There were also two inside the gym for winter, when the men stayed locked up more than they did in the summer.

In winter, there was no night yard; the men had to lock up as soon as they finished eating their last meal of the day. By six o'clock at night in the winter, there was no one out in the yard. You could see men hurrying across the yard, coming or going to school, then each block had a certain night for gym. Each block had its own basketball team, and most of the times, the ones not in the know bet on their block's team. Consequently, any man in the know could always make his cigarette money. If he knew who was good in chess or bridge, he could bet on those games, too. The prison paper carried the standings of the men in the chess clubs, so some inmates would bet on that week's chess games.

With his agile mind, Chester did easy time. He did the time; he didn't let the time do him. The years slipped by without his realizing where they had gone. His everyday program was never interrupted by stays in the hole. He could anticipate from past experience whenever a shakedown was due, so he was never caught dirty. He didn't read sex books, so he didn't worry about having them found in his cell.

"Hey, partner," Willie said to him one day as they walked towards the mess hall. "I got a chance to buy some mean spud juice, Chester. You want me to pick up a quart for you? If so, speak now or forever hold your peace."

Chester grinned, "Yeah, baby boy, how about picking up enough so that we can have us some before going to the movie tonight, then have a little bit left over to take to the movie. You cop the spud juice, and I'll pay our way to the movie, plus supply the potato chips and popcorn."

"That's cool, man. I'll just end up going in the hole about six packs of smokes, if you bothered to add up what the spud juice cost against what the chips and popcorn cost."

"Well, now," Chester stated as they reached the chow hall, "I ain't said nothing about the smokes you made when you bet on my chess game this morning, my friend. You didn't think I didn't know you had four boxes bet on me, did you?"

Both men hesitated as they reached the chow hall. There were two different lines, but both of them were long. On one side all the white men stood, on the other side, all the black men stood. For some reason, each group separated into these lines when they reached the mess hall. No one told them to line up this way, but the men did anyway. It was a tacit understanding between the black and white inmates; whites ate on their side, blacks on the other. Here and there you could see a black face in the white line, so the same thing in the black line. Most of the times, these were homosexuals, going to chow with their men. Sometimes it was just friends, men who worked on the same jobs came from work together and decided to eat together, but it was rare. Most of the times, black and white friends would end up separating at the chow line. It brought too much attention down on the inmate to eat in the wrong line. The officers on duty might get the wrong idea and think that those in the wrong color lines were homosexuals, so to keep the idle speculation off of them, the men quickly separated in the front of the mess hall.

Impatiently, Willie and Chester stopped and stared at the long line of men waiting for the door of the mess hall to open. "Fuck this shit!" Willie said, almost reading Chester's mind. "I ain't got enough time left on my sentence to stand in that long-ass line."

Chester grinned, then led the way around to the back of the mess hall. They jumped up on the garbage rack and went through the back door. They had to knock on the back door until one of the men working in the clipper room glanced out to see who it was. The men who worked in the mess hall were allowed to eat on the early line, but most of the time Chester and Willie, who worked in the kitchen, too, missed the early line because the inmate foreman might be short of help and then he'd grab whoever he saw to use on the job that needed filling.

As they grabbed their trays, Chester inquired, "What's that shit about you're too short? You don't think these peckerwoods are going to let you out on parole, do you?"

"Well I don't know, but you can damn well bet that when I go before the parole board next month, I'll be hoping like hell that they do." Instantly perspiration broke out on Willie's forehead. "I don't want to fool myself, Chester, but I just can't help it, man. It's all I think about, day and night. Before, my time was fast, but as soon as I found out that I was due to go before the board next month, man, I can't sleep, study, or even read a fuckin' book without my mind going back to the parole board."

An enormous feeling of anguish washed over Chester. Willie was so absorbed in his thoughts of freedom that he hadn't noticed the change in Chester. Impatiently, Chester tried to shake off the unwholesome feeling that had overcome him. He knew that he definitely resented the idea of Willie leaving. It was uncanny. He didn't understand it. It was too complicated, but he faced up to the reality of it. With exasperation, he realized that he was jealous. He had seen it happen dozens of times before, but in each instance he had felt that the man who resented his friend leaving was a petty bastard at heart. A real friend wouldn't resent his friend going home. In fact, he'd look forward to it. Just seeing a buddy going out should make a friend happy, so he had always thought, but now he knew differently.

"What's wrong, baby?" Willie asked at last, as they made their way through the chow line. "You don't like what's on the menu today?"

Chester managed to control his fleeting thoughts.

He was furious with himself because he knew that the first thing that had gone through his mind was the hope that Willie would get a flop at the board. "No, man, I was just thinking, wondering what you would do once you got out. You know that I know how your finances are, so I was hoping that once you got out, you wouldn't fuck around and end up taking off some bullshit caper that didn't have but three or four hundred dollars in it."

"Yeah, I know what you mean," Willie replied. He spotted a friend of theirs who worked in the mess hall. The man waved them over.

"What's happening, Albert?" Chester said as they joined the man. Albert Jones was one of those elite men in prison, one of those men who would never get out. He was a lifer, he had killed two policemen when they stopped his car one night. He had been drinking and arguing with his wife when the officers pulled him over. One thing led to another, and the policemen had ordered him out of the car. He got out shooting, killing the first officer instantly, then after the second one had fallen, he leaned over and pumped two shots into the officer's head. His wife had read the handwriting on the wall. She jumped out the other side of the car and ran, because she believed she would have been next—which was true. Albert had turned around and looked for her. Seeing her fleeing up the side of the hill on the expressway, he had taken aim and attempted to fire, only to find out that he had run out of bullets. By the time he had relieved one of the dead policemen of his gun, she was too far away for a pis-

tol. He had gone after her on foot, shooting at her
from a distance, but by the time he reached the top
of the hill, police cars were all over the place. His
wife rushed over to one, blurting out what had happened.

Albert didn't waste any time. He opened fire on the
police car, praying that he would hit her with a lucky
shot. He wasn't lucky, but he did wound another
policeman. By this time he was under fire and went
down with three bullets in his body. It was a wonder
that he lived. The doctors hadn't expected him to, but
somehow he survived.

"What it is? What it is?" he answered as they joined
him. "You guys look like you've got something cook-
ing. Maybe you've had some of that good spud juice
floating around, huh?"

The men set their trays down at his table and joined
him. "I wish we had some," Willie stated honestly,
then he turned to Chester and continued their earlier
conversation. "Naw, man, I didn't have anything
planned, Chester, but I was remembering a conversation we had where you were telling me about this joint
that sells food stamps. You said something about there
being something like thirty thousand dollars in the
joint, if I hit it at the right time."

Briefly, the men at the table fell silent, each for his
own reason. "Listen, Chester, if you pull my coat to
what I'd need to know, I'll go by your home and leave
your wife at least ten grand. I mean that, man, ten
grand, as soon as it's humanly possible. I know she
can use it for the kids, but if you didn't want me to

give her that much money, I'd give her five grand, then put the rest in the bank under your name—providing you're not out of prison by then."

Albert let out a whistle, "Boy, you guys are really dealing in big money this morning, goddamn! If I had that kind of dough, I'd be able to pay my way out of here."

Chester didn't say anything. He knew that no matter how much money Albert had, he wouldn't be able to pay his way out of prison. But each man had to have a dream of some kind, and that was Albert's dream: that someday, somehow, he'd come up with the money and be able to pay his way out.

When Willie started to go on talking about the robbery, Chester cut him off. "That's dead, Willie. They moved the joint. The last letter I got from my wife, she was telling me about how the stamp place moved." Chester caught Willie's eyes, warning him to shut up. He wished Willie hadn't said anything in front of Albert, even though he believed there was nothing Willie could say that Albert could use against them. After all, Albert was a dead man; they just hadn't put the dirt over his head yet. He was one of the walking dead.

The conversation changed at the table. The men began talking about the upcoming movie that night, about how many fine women there were in it. After the meal, Chester and Willie slipped out before the foreman could catch up with them. They hit the yard, stopped at the store—which sold pop and ice cream—ordered two pops, then continued walking around the

yard. They stopped over in the gambling area, where
the men bet two and three cartons on the turn of a
card. A man could either play poker or blackjack,
whichever game he preferred. The only thing that mattered was how much money he had to bet.

There was a high-stake table and a table for the
men who didn't have enough money to bet cartons.
There were dozens of games. Some inmates, the ones
who had been there for years, had private tables, tables
that they used every day. When they came to the yard
and someone was using their tables, the men had to
vacate. These were the big gamblers, the men who
could afford to hire a hit man inside the wall if it was
necessary. Sometimes it became necessary. A young
inmate sent down from one of the mad houses where
the young inmates were held because the prison
authorities couldn't control them, for example, might
see the old con raking in money at his table and try
and take over.

Then one night the prison guards would walk by
the showers, which were located on base, and find a
body or pass a cell and see a man stretched out on
his bunk, his neck at a funny angle. The word would
have already been passed up and down the tiles; men
would know that a hit was going on, but no one wanted any part of it. It didn't pay to be involved as a witness—not if one wanted to leave the prison alive—
because the inmates ran the prison. There was no
doubt about that. Just about everything that happened
or was going to happen inside the walls of the prison,
the prisoners knew long before the guards did.

16

THE DAY FINALLY arrived that Chester had dreaded. Willie had been before the parole board and had made it. Now he had received his slip informing him of his out day. He had been to dress-out and gotten fitted for the suit that he would wear home.

The morning that he was to leave, Chester walked to chow with him. They ate their breakfast quietly. Albert came from behind the chow line and joined them. Chester resented the intrusion but didn't say anything. There were so many things left to be talked about. He had hoped to use the time in the chow hall to finish up talking about certain things, but now he couldn't—not in front of a third person.

Willie didn't have the same caution. "Don't worry about nothing, Chester. Even though you got a flop at the board, you'll be out before long." Willie hesitated for a second, then added, "Besides, partner, by the time you've finished jailing, I'll have done took off that joint and we'll be rolling in dough. We can go to Mexico and party when you get out, man. You ain't got nothing to worry about. I got the problem; I got to rip off the joint. All you got to do is sit here and wait. You'll hear it on the news, then you'll know we're on our way. Big money, fine bitches, a laid Cadillac. How about that? I might even buy you a beautiful, red Caddie drop-top, at that." Willie was too busy with his dreams as he talked to notice the anger in Chester's face. He didn't bother to stop talking long enough to find out what was on Chester's mind.

"Hold on, baby," Chester said, interrupting the flow of words. "You keep talking, and you'll have Albert here really believing we got something going on."

Willie glanced up, surprised. "We have got something going on, and it ain't no Mickey Mouse job, either," Willie said without thinking.

After all these years, Chester thought to himself, I finally find out I've been fuckin' with a fool.

"Aw, man," Albert said quickly, "you ain't got to worry about snowing me. I ain't nobody."

Chester got up from the table without finishing his food. "I ain't trying to snow nobody," he said heatedly. "And I don't know what the fuck all the bullshit is about. Willie is just trying to bullshit you, Albert, like we got something big up, but we ain't got nothing going." With that, Chester turned and walked away.

Willie got up quickly and followed him out. "What's the matter, man? We're too close for you to come down on me like that. Why you want to make the guy think I'm a liar, man?" Willie was really dumbfounded by Chester's action.

"Goddamn it, Willie, what the fuck's wrong with you? I thought you had more on the ball than that! I wish the fuck I hadn't said anything to you about that job, man. Here you sit in the mess hall and run your goddamn game in front of a man who doesn't have anything going for him. He'll jump at any kind of straw to get out, even if it didn't happen or it couldn't help him. He'll still run up front and tell them people if he thought it would do him any good. I thought you had more sense than that! Really I did! Now, I don't know. I really just don't know." Chester shook his head. He was astonished by Willie's thoughtlessness. "Why don't we just call the whole thing off, Willie. Let it ride until I get out. You have got to have help on the job anyway, so just wait until I'm home. Then we'll take it off together."

Moisture stood out on Willie's forehead. He realized now how foolish he must have sounded, but it was the excitement of going home and everything that had made him run off with the lip. He started to explain this to Chester, then decided not to because of his shame. He didn't want to give Chester the idea this late in the game that he was a kid who couldn't control his mouth, so a silence fell between them, one that was to last until they said their farewells.

Chester helped Willie carry his belongings over to the front office. They shook hands silently. After all these years together, this was really the first time they had ever had any kind of disagreement. "Remember now," Chester began, "just hold on until I come home. It ain't but nine more months, then we'll hit the joint together. That way can't nothing go wrong, you know what I mean?"

Willie agreed, but in the back of his mind the thought began to take shape to pull the job off as soon as possible, just so that he could show Chester that he wasn't a poot-butt.

After Willie took his stuff and walked on towards dress-out Chester stood and stared after him. He had a premonition. He didn't feel right about something. He knew that he was safe, but he worried about Willie. He liked the young man. If only he'll wait, Chester said over and over again as he stalked back towards his cell. He pushed open his door and slammed it closed behind him. The only way he could get out now was to catch a guard whenever one came by, checking out the empty cells. At this time of day most men would be at work. In fact, Chester suddenly realized that he should have been at work himself. They had cornflakes that morning, so he should have been there, taking care of the bowls.

*   *   *

Willie didn't waste any time getting set up for the job. He got two of his high-school friends to help him—Rayfield, whose real name was Charles Roman, and a short skinny dope fiend named Jake Hawkins, sometimes called Tiny.

The men entered the food-stamp place at twelve o'clock sharp. Some of the clerks had taken off for lunch, but the security guard was still on duty. It was Jake's job to take care of the guard. At first the situation was theirs; they had it under control, but Jake made a mistake. Instead of taking the guard's gun, he only held the guard at bay.

Suddenly a woman entered the front door; she was fat and dark-complexioned. As soon as she saw what was going on, she screamed. "I'm not about to let you bastards take my money," she yelled, then struck out with her purse.

Rayfield was the man nearest her. When she struck his arm, the gun went off. The bullet hit her right in the stomach. She clutched at her stomach, surprise spread all over her face, then slumped to the floor, murmuring over and over again, "I'm shot. I'm shot."

The momentary silence that fell over the place didn't last long. Willie had been busy collecting the money, but the shot caused him a dilemma that he wasn't capable of really handling. Willie was a follower, not a leader. His mind didn't function fast enough; furthermore, he had picked the wrong kind of men for the job. After Rayfield fired the shot, they panicked. Jake, thinking only of himself, broke and ran. He forgot he had left the guard with his gun. As soon as he turned his back on the guard, the guard pulled his pistol. The sound was loud in the small confines of the building.

Jake's body jerked from the striking power of the slug that tore into his back. Willie gritted his teeth as he raised his pistol and shot the guard in the head. It was a matter of fight or die. He had decided to fight. Willie grabbed the small black bag he had been stuffing with money and leaped the counter. He broke and ran for the door. Rayfield beat him out the door.

A police car pulled up as soon as the fleeing men were leaving the building. The officer on the passenger side shot through his open window without getting out of the car. The bullet lifted Rayfield off his feet, and he fell back against Willie. The jolt jarred the gun from Willie's hand. As Willie scrambled around trying to pick up the gun, the policemen rushed up.

"If you touch it, you're a dead man!" one of them yelled. Willie stopped searching for the gun. As he lay down on the ground, the thought flashed across his mind that he hadn't been out of prison thirty days. Not even a full month; tears came to his eyes at the thought of it.

* * *

The news came over the radio that evening. As Chester lay on his bunk smoking with his earphones on, he heard it and cursed. "You damn fool, Willie, I told you to wait, goddamn it. I begged you to wait, but no, hell no, you had to be the fuckin' big shot! You couldn't wait!"

All that night he lay awake, struggling with his conscience; if it hadn't been for his telling Willie about it, it would never have happened. He could visualize

Willie now, lying in some filthy bull pen, waiting for the morning when they would arraign him for murder. Finally with the maturity of fatalism, Chester realized that it was out of his hands. The best he could do would be to send Willie some cigarettes, maybe drop him a card every Christmas or so. He believed that he would be out of prison before Willie ever hit the prison yard, so he doubted if they would ever see each other again.

But he was wrong.

Two days later, when two detectives came inside the prison to talk to him, Chester knew he was in trouble. He didn't realize how much, but he knew it was big trouble. The first friend he had ever had, his first rap partner, so to speak, had involved him in the robbery. The very next day, when the daily newspapers reached the prison, the headlines carried the story:

ROBBERY MASTERMINDED
BY INMATE IN PRISON

Chester stayed at Jackson until the trial came up. He was just about due to go home on discharge when they came to get him. He had talked to his public defender many times, so he knew just what he was fighting. He was fighting a first-degree murder charge, and he had never left prison. Because of the killings involved, his case was a big one. Front page news. The newspapermen were crowded in the courtroom waiting when they brought Chester down. The case had already begun. They only brought Chester down when it was time for him to appear.

The deputies that brought him down led him to a bull pen. There they took off his handcuffs. As soon as they left, his lawyer rushed up to the bars. "Damn it, Hines, I asked you to be honest with me about this!"

Chester stared at his lawyer as if he had lost his mind. "I have been honest with you. I told Willie not to rob that joint. I swear to it."

The lawyer stared at him coldly. "All right, Mr. Hines, then what about this guy, Jones, Albert Jones, I think his name is? He's a lifer in Jackson. He says he heard you guys planning this robbery on more than one occasion. In fact, he says the morning that this Willie character was getting out of prison, you were telling him the final details of this robbery. Is that correct?"

Suddenly it was too much.. Chester couldn't even concentrate. To get a case like this was too much. To damn near be found guilty was too much to believe. It just couldn't happen, yet it was happening.

"Man, listen, please. I'm telling you the truth. Albert is a lifer. He'll do anything, tell any kind of lie, if he believes it's possible that it will help him get out. I don't know why Willie is involving me, but man, I asked that kid not to do it. Yes, we talked about it. The same way we talked about robbing a dozen banks, but it was just bullshit, something to pass the time away with."

The lawyer shook his head and walked away. Later on that morning they came and got Chester. When he entered the courtroom, Willie looked every way but in his direction. He couldn't look Chester in the eye.

When Chester finally took the stand, he looked straight at Willie and asked, "Why, Willie, why? Why would you do this to me?" Again Willie looked away. Shame was written across his face. As the days of the trial wore on, Chester began to struggle with a full-blown hatred. Between the two men, Albert and Willie, Chester didn't know who he hated the most. He couldn't stand the sight of either one of them. He knew that, if he were ever near one of them in prison, he'd kill the man, regardless of the outcome.

A blackness enveloped him the day the jury came in with a verdict of guilty. Chester couldn't believe that twelve people had found him guilty as charged. He wanted to scream out to them that it wasn't fair. He was in prison at the time, how could he be guilty of murder when he was four hundred miles away?

The morning they took him over for sentence, he had to stifle a recurring thought. This was the date that he would have been coming home from prison, free, discharged—not on parole but completely finished with his jail term. But instead, because he had allowed himself to become friendly with another human being, he was going to court to be sentenced.

When he reached the courtroom, heavily hand-cuffed, he had to make his mind a blank. Willie had already been sentenced; he had heard through the grapevine that Willie had received forty to fifty years in prison. Now he was going for his turn. He stood in front of the judge, trying desperately to merely

exist, to stifle his thoughts, not to scream out how
unfair it was. When the judge asked him if he was
ready for sentence and if he had anything to say before
sentencing, he could only shake his head. What good
were words now, he thought. He had said everything
he could possibly say during the trial. What could he
add now when it wouldn't make any difference? He
could only shake his head.

The judge looked down at him from his bench.
"Chester Hines," he said in a voice Chester thought
awfully deep for such a small man, "I sentence you
to life in prison."

Life in prison. Chester was stunned. He stood
motionless for what seemed an eternity as the judge's
voice reverberated in his mind: life in prison..., life
in prison..., life in prison....

Donald Goines
SPECIAL PREVIEW

WHORESON
The Story of
A Ghetto Pimp

This excerpt from Whoreson: The Story of a Ghetto Pimp *will introduce you to one of Donald Goines' most interesting characters—Whoreson Jones, son of a beautiful black prostitute and an unknown white john. By the age of sixteen, Whoreson is a full-fledged pimp, cold-blooded, ruthless. Written in gritty street talk,* Whoreson *is a story that offers a startling glimpse into the hell of the inner city, yet it bristles with bitter humor and defiant pride.*

1

FROM WHAT I HAVE been told it is easy to imagine the cold, bleak day when I was born into this world. It was December 10, 1940, and the snow had been falling continuously in Detroit all that day. The cars moved slowly up and down Hastings Street, turning the white flakes into slippery slush. Whenever a car stopped in the middle of the street, a prostitute would get out of it or a whore would dart from one of the darkened doorways and get into the car.

Jessie, a tall black woman with high, narrow cheekbones, stepped from a trick's car holding her stomach. Her dark piercing eyes were flashing with anger. She began cursing the driver, using the vilest language imaginable about his parents and the nature of his birth. The driver, blushing with shame, drove away, leaving her behind in the falling snow. Slush from the spinning tires spattered her as she held onto a parked car for support. She unconsciously rubbed her hand across her face to wipe away the tears that mingled with the snowflakes.

Two prostitutes standing across the street in the Silver-line doorway, an old dilapidated bar that catered to hustling girls, watched her curiously.

Before she could move, another car stopped behind her. She turned and stared at the white face leering over the steering wheel. The driver noticed as she turned that her stomach was exceptionally large. Guessing her condition, he drove on. She stood holding her stomach and watching the car move down the street until it stopped near a group of women in front of a bar. She started to move towards the sidewalk, but her legs gave out on her, and she fell into the slush in the street.

From the darkened doorways, prostitutes of various complexions ran to the stricken woman's aid. Before, where there had been closed windows, there now appeared heads of different shapes and sizes.

"Bring that crazy whore up here," a stout woman yelled from a second-story window. While four women half carried and half dragged Jessie up the stairs, a young girl, still in her teens, yelled to the woman in the window, "I think she goin' have that damn baby, Big Mama."

The large woman in the window looked down at

the girl, amused. "It's about time she had it, gal. Seems she been sticking out for a whole year." Big Mama started to close the window, then added, "You run down the street and get that nigger doctor, gal, and don't stop for no tricks."

The young girl started off for the doctor, muttering under her breath. She ducked her head and pulled up her collar in an attempt to cut off the chilling wind. When a car stopped and the driver blew his horn, she ignored the call for business and continued on her errand.

Big Mama's living room was full of prostitutes sitting and standing around, gossiping. It was rare for a woman to have a baby on the streets; also, it gave them an excuse to come in out of the snow.

"What the hell Jessie working out in this kind of weather for? Ain't she and her man saved no money?" a short, brown-skinned, dimpled woman asked. The room became quiet until another woman spoke up.

"You know goddamn well that black ass bastard she had for a pimp run off last week with some white whore," she said harshly. "He jumped on Jessie and took all the money she been saving to get in the hospital with, too."

This comment started up gossip on the merits of various pimps—then suddenly a slap and the sound of a baby yelling came to them, and everyone became silent.

Big Mama put out the few girls who had remained in the bedroom, then took the baby from the doctor and carried it towards the bed. Her large face was aglow with happiness as she smiled at the woman lying in her bed.

"You can be glad of one thing, Jessie, this baby don't belong to that nigger of yours that's gone," she said while turning the baby around so the mother could see it. "Looks like you done went and got you a trick baby, honey, but for a child as black as you, I sure don't see how you got one this light."

Jessie raised herself and stared at the bundle Big Mama held. "Oh my God," she cried and fell back onto the bed. Big Mama stepped back from the bed, shocked, and held the baby tighter. Her dark face, just a shade lighter than Jessie's, was filled with concern. She had never had a child of her own. Like many women who have been denied offspring, she had an overwhelming love for children. Her voice took on a tone that all of the prostitutes working out of her house respected. When she spoke this way they listened, perhaps because she weighed over three hundred pounds and had been known to knock down men with one swing of her huge hands. She spoke and only her voice could be heard in the house.

"If you don't want this baby, Jessie, I'll take him." Her eyes were full of tears as she looked down at the tiny bundle in her arms. "You can damn well bet he'll have good taking care of, too."

The small, elderly, balding doctor cleared his throat. He held out a birth certificate. "I'll have to get on to my other calls, so please give me a name for the little fat fellow."

Jessie stared at the bundle Big Mama held. All the

black curls covering the baby's head only inflamed her anger. Her eyes were filled with blind rage as she turned and stared at the doctor. He stepped back unconsciously. Here, he thought, was a woman who had been badly misused by some man. He hoped that he would never again see so much hate in a woman's eyes.

Jessie laughed suddenly, a cold, nerve-tingling sound. Big Mama shivered with fear, not for herself, but for the tiny life she held in her arms.

"Well, Mrs. Jones," the doctor inquired, "have you decided on what to call your baby?"

"Of course, doc, I've got just the name for the little sonofabitch—Whoreson, Whoreson Jones."

The doctor looked as if he had been struck by lightning. His mouth gaped, and he stared at her dumbfounded.

Big Mama was the first to recover. "You can't do that, Jessie. Give the child a good Christian name."

"Christian name hell!" Jessie replied sharply. "I'm naming my son just what he is. I'm a whore and he's my son. If he grows up ashamed of me, the hell with him. That's what I'm wantin' to name him, and that's what it's goin' to be. Whoreson!"

2

THE SLUM I GREW UP in seemed to me to be the most wonderful place in the world. My early childhood was pleasant and it was a rare occasion when I saw something in a store that my mother couldn't buy for me. Jessie saw to it that I always had money for the candy store. Whenever I lost the marbles she had previously bought, she'd quickly give me money to buy some more. Most of us kids loved the backyards and alleys that we played in with our slingshots made out of discarded tire tubes. We overturned garbage cans in the hope of startling a good-sized rat so we could shoot at it with our homemade slingshots. Between the alley cats, dogs and us, we kept the alleys, yards, and rundown barns clean of rats during summer daylight hours. When night fell it was the other side of the coin. The rats came out in full force, and many children were bitten because they had slept out on the porch to beat the evening heat.

We lived in an upper flat on the second floor. Besides my mother and me, there was a big tomcat that we just called "Cat" who shared the flat with us. Before Jessie would go to work at night, she always managed to run Cat down and toss him in my bed with me. For me to mention sleeping out on the front porch at night was taboo, so I would play with Cat in my large bed until I fell asleep. I didn't know it at the time, but she did it because of her fear of rats. After tucking me into the bed she would ruffle my hair and kiss me on the cheek.

"Well, little pimp, I got to go and catch 'em now. You be good and I'll let you count the trap money in the morning," she'd say before turning out the light and leaving me on my own until she came back some-time in the morning.

On a few occasions she didn't get back in the morning. When this occurred one of my mother's girl-friends would be in the bed with me when I woke up. When this happened, I'd know that Jessie wouldn't be home until later that day, so I would go downstairs and have my breakfast. The woman who lived under us had a bunch of children, so one more mouth didn't make too much difference. When we played in the backyard the boys next door would call them the wel-fare's pride and joy. If I'd laugh too much, the little girls who stayed under me would remark, "Ain't no sense you laughing, fool, 'cause your mammy ain't nothing but a whore."

I'd look at them and grin. "You're the fool, girl. You and your sisters and mammy need to get off welfare and become whores." This would cause all of the kids in the yard to laugh and I'd join in with them. At the age of five it's pretty hard for a child to understand the meaning of "whore."

If my mother wasn't home after I ate lunch, I'd wait till the woman upstairs woke up, and then she'd take me over to Big Mama's to stay. This made me think I was the most fortunate boy in the world. Instead of one mother, I had two. Big Mama and Jessie.

With the passing of summer my small world began to change. A big event in my life was my first trip to the neighborhood barbershop. Jessie dressed me with care. She had me put on my new suit and shoes, then marched me out of the house. She had always cut my hair at home, but since I was going to start school in the fall, she decided to have it done at the barbershop. The men sitting around the place stared at us when we entered. I didn't care. The barbershop was a foreign place to me. I stared around in wonder. The tall chairs with men sitting in them getting their hair combed, the glittering mirrors that surrounded the walls, all of this was a new world for me. The loud music from the jukebox made my feet sway with the beat, as I danced along beside Jessie, keeping up.

She seemed unconcerned as she walked me up to

an empty chair. She spoke to a short, fat, balding barber. "I want you to cut it off the back real good, but
don't take much off the top."

The barber sighed, "Why is it, girl, every time one
of ya bring in a red nigger, you always say just cut a
little off, but when you bring in a black boy, you want
it all cut off."

Jessie stared at him coldly. "Nigger, all you got to
do is look at your head in the mirror, then look at his
hair. But that ain't here nor there. I ain't got nothing
to do with how you cut some little black boy's hair.
What I'm worried about is how you cut my little red
nigger's hair. So you pay heed, nigger, this red one is
mine, and you cut it like I say." She whirled on her
heel and stalked out.

The men lounging in the shop laughed loudly. One
heavy-voiced man roared over the noise. "I'll bet you
cut that boy's hair right, Lew." Lew seemed to take
it as a joke. He smiled, displaying a row of yellow
stained teeth. "That's just what I was telling you boys
the other day. A nigger couldn't give me no black
woman. They is the most meanest woman God ever
put breath in." He continued, "You damn near got to
be crazy to fight with Jessie anyway. She fights like
a man."

Another bystander spoke up. "Shit, man, consider
yourself lucky if she fights and don't do no cutting.
That black girl there is sure'nuff mean with a razor."

The barber rubbed my head the way Jessie did
sometimes before he started to trim my hair. After he
finished with my haircut he bought me a pop and sat

me up on top of the shoeshine stand. "I wonder where your ma went?" he asked offhandedly.

One of the idle bystanders spoke up. "She probably caught a trick, Lew." Lew shook his head for the man to remain silent, but the man continued. "Hell, Lew, don't you never think that boy don't know what his mother does. Ask him what his name is."

"I know what his name is," Lew answered. I was too young to understand the pity the man had for me, but his kindness was understood.

Jessie came through the door, walking as though the world belonged to her. Her high-heeled shoes rang louder than the taps on my heels as she took that long stride of hers. She stopped and swayed, her hands on her hips. Every eye in the barbershop was on this tall black woman who carried herself wlth such pride. "Well, Lew, I guess I won't have to make you knock down one of these walls getting out of here this time."

Lew grinned. "I'm sure glad you ain't goin' to do me no harm, Jess. I sure started to cut a little more off the top, though. You damn near got this boy looking like a girl with all this hair on his head."

Jessie reached up and removed me from the shoeshine stand. She picked me up with the same ease that Lew had shown.

"I'm glad you didn't, Lew," she said. "I know how I want my pimp's hair to look, and this is the only pimp I got." With a vigorous shove, Jessie started me towards the door. I ran out of the shop into the street I loved so well. There was not much difference between the daylight business and the night business on Hastings. The street was full of slow-moving cars, the drivers being more interested in the colored prostitutes in the doorways than on the traffic moving in front of them. I waved at the various girls I knew standing in the gangways. Some of them yelled across the street at me. "Look at Whoreson, ain't he sharp today!"

Jessie caught up with me. "You take your fast ass home and get out of them new clothes." I crossed the street on my way home, and one of the girls came out of a doorway and caught me. She gave me a hug, then pressed a quarter into my hand.

"Let that boy go on home, ya ain't doing nothing but spoiling him," Jessie yelled. I grinned, kissed the girl on the cheek, and went home.

3

MY FIRST DAYS IN school were uneventful except for the shock my first name had for my teachers. Of course they quickly solved this problem by simply using my last name. However, this didn't stop my classmates from calling me Whoreson on all occasions, causing my teachers to curse my mother's choice of names. At this stage of life, school was wonderful. On the way to school we used to steal from the delivery trucks making their morning stops.

On a few occasions some prostitute who was still up working, or just coming out, would yell at me, "I'm telling your mammy on you, boy, if you steal that junk."

I don't know if they ever told, but if they did, Jessie never said anything about it. Because the whores always yelled at me, it made me popular with my gang. They commented on the fact that all the prostitutes on Hastings knew me.

My best friend, Tony, would put his arm around my shoulder. His mother sometimes worked with Jessie, so we spent a lot of time together. "Me and you, Whoreson," he would say, "we goin' to be the best pimps in the whole goddamn world."

I would look up at Tony's dark face and grin. He was taller than me, and I was tall for my age. Tony could outrun, plus outfight, anybody in our gang except Ape. Everybody knew couldn't nobody whip Ape. He was big, dumb, and strong. There were a lot of grown men who wouldn't tangle with Ape.

We always waited on the corner in the mornings for everybody in our gang before going on to school. If somebody wasn't going, there was always some kid in the gang who knew about it. Tony would stop by for me, then we would stop and get Ape. This way, everybody came to the corner with somebody. After nine or ten of us got together we would start for school, looking for something to steal on the way.

After my ninth birthday I began to really understand the meaning of my name. I began to understand just what my mother was doing for a living. There was nothing I could do about it, but even had I been able to, I wouldn't have changed it.

There was a boy in our gang named Milton, whose mother wouldn't allow Tony or me in her house. She

didn't even really want her son to play with us, but
he found out it was easier to run with us than to get
whipped on the way to school every day. I once heard
her yell at him while we were waiting on the sidewalk:

"Milton, if I catch you giving that junkie bitch's
son some of your candy, I'll kill you when you get
home. That goes for that little half-white nigger they
call Whoreson, too. You hear me boy? I mean it now,
you take this quarter and save some change for
school."

It had been Tony's idea that Milton try and get some
money so we could buy some candy. After Milton
bought the candy, Tony wouldn't eat any. He told
Milton to take it home and stick it down his mother's
big mouth. I helped Milton eat up the candy. She
wasn't the first person who had said something about
me, nor did I think she would be the last. To tell the
truth, I enjoyed eating it, because I knew she didn't
want me to have it. Tony seemed so pitiful watching
me eat the candy that I suggested we stop at Big
Mama's. If she didn't give us any money, she'd sure
have something to eat. I wasn't hungry but I knew
Tony was. It seemed as if his mother never did cook,
'cause he was always hungry.

Milton started to complain. "Ya'll know I can't go
up there, Whoreson. You done ate up all my candy,
now you don't want me to be with you."

I saw a girl from my class at school going down
Hastings Street, and I started to run to catch up with
her. "Come on if you ain't scared," I yelled back at

Milton.

Tony ran beside me and laughed at Milton. "Come on, punk, you might get a chance to see somebody doing it, if you don't be so frightened of your mother." We crossed the street at a dead run, causing a driver to slam on his brakes. He stuck his head out the window and cursed loudly, but it just made us to laugh.

Janet turned and saw us coming, but before she could get away I had grabbed her and felt where her tits should have been, if she had had any. She called me a nasty thing and tried to hit me, but I danced back out of the way. Tony came up behind her, grabbed her by the ass, then jumped back. She screamed and slapped out at him, but she was too slow. He joined me and we laughed. We had started on down the street when two whores stepped out of a gangway and caught us from behind. Before we could break loose, Janet had run up and slapped both of us. Tony tried to kick her, but the woman holding him got mad and slapped him upside the head harder than Janet ever could have.

"Keep your black ass feet on the ground, little nigger, you hear?" she commanded. Tony complied by keeping his feet still.

Not wanting to appear frightened, I resorted to threats. "When I catch you in school, Janet, I'm going to do more than that."

Janet shook her little skinny hips at me. "You ain't goin' to do nothin', nigger, but try and get along with me," she answered. I tried to get free but the woman held me tighter. "You just wait and see," I yelled. "First time I catch you in school I'm goin' stick it in your little tight puss."

Both of the women who had seized us laughed. The one holding Tony remarked gaily, "Just listen to them. Ain't neither one of 'em got enough to stick in a pop bottle."

I turned bright red, blushing down to my toes. Tony was on the case, though, and he capped sharply, "We got enough to bust your big wide ass open, woman."

Instead of making them angry, his remark only amused them. Then suddenly we heard a voice roar from the window above us.

Big Mama was leaning out of the window. "Bring them fresh little niggers up here. I'm goin' to see how long it's goin' be before they feel on another little girl in the streets."

On hearing the sound of Big Mama's voice, plus seeing that look in her eyes, we really tried to get free. It was useless, though, because after she finished speaking some more girls helped the first two to carry us upstairs.

When we got upstairs Big Mama bore down on us. Both of us were shaking so bad we couldn't get our lies straight. I tried to explain that we were not feeling Janet, just playing with her. For telling this lie, I got a well-placed slap. After that, the women got together and took our pants off. A white man coming out of the back bedroom stopped and gave Big Mama his belt. She took the belt and lit us up with it. After we had begged, cried and pleaded, plus called her

Grandma, she gave us our pants back and sent us into the kitchen to eat.

After eating some ham hocks and greens, we tried to beg some money out of Big Mama. She promised us another beating if we didn't get out of her sight, so we ran down the stairs. The long narrow stairway was dimly lit, so we didn't see the two women who had grabbed us until we got to the bottom. They stood in the dilapidated doorway laughing at us. Tony asked the one who had grabbed him to give up a quarter. She gave him a personal invitation to go to hell, so I tried another approach. I promised the one who had caught me a kiss if she would give up the coin.

She stared at me for a moment. "Give me one good reason why I should want to kiss you," she said, "and I'll give you a quarter."

I stared straight into her eyes and stated, "Since I'm just a little pimp all I'm asking for is a quarter, but you know all you whores love to give pimps money, so just give it up, whore."

Her mouth flew open and she just stared. I stepped back out of the way. I knew Jessie had told all of her girlfriends to pop me upside the head whenever they heard me swear, so I wasn't taking no chances.

The sound of men laughing caused me to turn. I saw two men sitting in a Cadillac who I knew had to be real pimps. They were wearing silk suits and their hair was beautifully processed.

One of the men called over the girl I had been talking to. He gave her two dollars and pointed at us. "You give it to them," he said. "That way they can say they really got some whore money."

She came back from the car and gave Tony his dollar. She held mine in her hand. "You owe me something," she said and leaned down.

I caught Tony's eye. He nodded towards her breast.
I winked at him and stood on my toes. I put my hand
with the dollar in it around her neck, then kissed her
on the mouth. She stuck her tongue into my mouth;
my eyes opened in surprise. Reaching up with my
empty hand, I squeezed her left breast. I ducked my
head to miss the blow, if one was coming, before she
could move. Tony moved in behind her fast, sticking
his hand as high up under her dress as it would go.
She screamed and we ran down the street laughing.
Tony yelled to me, "Whoreson, she ain't got no draw-
ers on." People walking down the street stopped and
laughed, Big Mama yelled out of the window at us,
and the pimps in the car roared with laughter. The
other prostitute broke out in a run after us, but when
we cut into a gangway that led into an alley she
stopped.

After this experience Tony and I stayed on
Hastings. When we were on this street of excitement,
everything seemed to happen, life was full. Perhaps
our introduction to vice was premature for our age,
but it prepared us well for our chosen profession. My
mother tried hard during this period to stop me from
hanging around poolrooms and trick-houses. Her beatings were useless, though. She even tried using coat
hangers twisted together. She called them her "pimp
sticks" and used them only when I had been excep-

tionally bad. Even after she had used coat hangers, I wouldn't stay off the corner. For two or three days after a severe beating I would stay close to the house, but when you're young and wild, you soon forget the whippings, or just try not to get caught next time.

Tony had started staying at my house four nights out of a week, so Jessie whipped him as much as she did me. After I turned ten she began to see that beatings were not the answer. She discontinued them, except for when we would sneak back out after she went to work. For some reason she couldn't stand for me to see her working on the streets.

At school our gang had become a terror. We shook down all the kids our age, plus a few of the older ones. We took their lunch money daily, until one day we beat up two brothers who had rebelled against our extortion. Their mother came back to school with the police. The principal informed the officers that Tony and I were the ringleaders. We denied this, but it didn't do any good.

The detectives wouldn't believe our lies, so we ended up by being escorted home by them. Tony said we were half-brothers and lived together. I think he told this lie to stop them from going to his house, where they might have found narcotics lying around.

When the police knocked, Jessie had to get out of the bed to open the door. She just stood there staring at us when the officer pushed us through the door. After listening to the police talk, her eyes began to shoot sparks. We knew there was big trouble ahead.

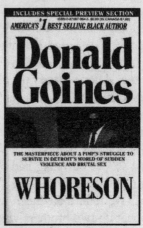